The AMAZING DAYS of ABBY HAYES

Have Wheels, Will Travel

ANNE MAZER

AN
APPLE
PAPERBACK

SCHOLASTIC INC.
New York Toronto London Auckland Sydney
Mexico City New Delhi Hong Kong

For Kevin C.

Thanks to Kerry, who told me about broken arms, and to Casey, who endured one. (No, Natalie isn't you!) Thanks to Katie and Rachel, who enlightened me about hamster toys; to Geoffrey, who suggested tea and marmalade; and to Tamar for the Spanish tutorial. As always, thanks to Mollie, who <u>never</u> runs out of ideas!

ISBN 0-439-34123-X

12 11 10 9 8 7   3 4 5 6/0

Printed in the U.S.A.   40

First Scholastic Book Club printing, January 2002

Chapter 1

Who wants a horse with wings? I want a pair of Rollerblades on my feet!

It's sixty-two degrees outside. The snow has melted. Spring is here! Our whole family is going to the lake this afternoon. There's an eight-mile path for jogging, biking, and Rollerblading. My Rollerblades are too small, so Eva gave me her old ones. I'm going to race Alex. I bet I beat him.

"Come on, Alex, hurry up," Abby Hayes said to her seven-year-old brother. "Shut that thing off."

"What? Oh, okay," Alex said, barely listening. He was playing a new computer game. "I have to beat this level."

"Which one are you on?"

"Seventy-six." The screen lit up. "Yes! I got to seventy-seven!" he yelled.

"Pretty good," Abby said, even though she had no idea what he was talking about. "You have to stop playing now. We're almost ready to leave. Dad's downstairs loading up the car. Are you even dressed?"

It looked like Alex had slept in his clothes. He had probably played the game in his sleep, too.

Abby touched his arm. "Come on, Alex, quit the game."

"Okay," Alex replied, without taking his eyes off the screen. "I'll just save first." Menus appeared and disappeared as Alex clicked the mouse rapidly. Abby couldn't follow what he was doing. Then the screen went blank.

"Finally!" she said. "Now, get yourself cleaned up."

With one hand, Alex combed through his tousled hair with his fingers; with the other, he shoved his shirt into his sweatpants.

If Alex wore all his clothes inside out or even upside down, he would never notice. If he had chocolate smeared on his face or one sneaker and one sandal on his feet, he wouldn't see it, either. His brain was full of math problems, computer games, designs for robots, and science questions.

"Get your Rollerblades," Abby told him. "Or do you want to ride your bike?"

"Rollerblades," Alex answered. He had just gotten new ones.

"I'll race you," Abby said. "The winner buys the loser an ice cream."

"No, if you win, I'll buy you an ice cream," Alex said. "If I win, you have to play chess with me."

Abby made a face. Alex *always* won at chess. It wasn't fun having a seven-year-old genius brother who could beat you no matter what.

"Come on, Abby," Alex begged. "Please!"

"Oh, all right," she grumbled. "Are you sure you'd rather play chess than eat ice cream?"

"Uh-huh." Alex picked up a gym bag from his closet floor.

"Do you have your helmet and pads? Mom said to make sure you had everything."

He pointed to the gym bag. "Yep."

The car horn sounded.

"We're coming!" Abby yelled out the window. They ran down the stairs to the minivan.

"We have a car full of Rollerbladers here," Paul Hayes said, as they headed for the lake. "Except for your mother and myself, of course."

Abby's father had put his bike on the roof of the van. Her mother was going to jog alongside him. She always ran, even in the winter. Sometimes she even raced in marathons.

"You should get Rollerblades, Mom and Dad," Eva urged. She pulled her hair back from her face with a plain rubber band. "It's so much fun; you'd love it!"

Abby's older SuperSis Eva loved just about every sport imaginable. She was captain of half a dozen teams and the star of them all. The number one on the back of her basketball jersey summed it up; when it came to athletics, Eva ruled.

"It looks like fun," their mother agreed. "But you know how much I love running. If I ever get sick of it, I'll rent Rollerblades and try them out."

"It's easier on your joints, Mom," Isabel said. She

was Eva's twin, but no one who knew them ever believed they were related. While Eva spent her time shooting hoops, swimming laps, and pitching shutouts, Isabel was in the library or on the computer doing research. She could tell you about the Hundred Years' War, the War of the Roses, and any other war you didn't want to know about.

The twins looked nothing alike, either. Today both were going to Rollerblade: Eva wore gray sweats, while Isabel wore bright spandex tights and a tank top.

"Rollerblading is better for your body," Isabel continued. "Unless you fall, of course."

"That's right," Eva said. "Listen to what Isabel is saying, Mom and Dad."

"You two agree?" Abby said.

Eva and Isabel nodded.

Abby grabbed her journal.

Shock waves rolled through the Hayes vehicle as Isabel Hayes and Eva Hayes, age fourteen, <u>actually agreed</u>.

The last time this happened was one day after they were born, when both were hun-

gry at the same time. Since then, the twin
SuperSisters have agreed on <u>nothing</u>. They
do not wear the same clothes, eat the same
food, or think the same thoughts.

The only thing they have in common is
SuperSisdom. Eva is brawn; Isabel is
brain. The Terrific Twins conquer the world.
Between them, they are better at everything
than everyone.

There was a moment of awed silence as
Paul and Olivia Hayes and the two non-
twins, Abby and Alex, contemplated the su-
pernatural event that had just taken place.
If the twins agreed, what
next? Chickens falling from the
sky?
Aliens tap dancing on the
highway?

Or . . . INTERRUPTION! This bulletin
has been interrupted by a lively discussion.
Are elbow and knee pads necessary for
Rollerblading? Eva says no, only wrist
guards and a helmet. Isabel says the more
protection, the safer the sport.

Olivia Hayes, mother, lawyer, and long-

distance runner, pronounces the
final word: "Everyone in the
Hayes family must wear bike
helmet, wrist, elbow, and knee
pads when they Rollerblade."

Isabel smug about victory; Eva furious.
"A good athlete doesn't have accidents,"
she says. "Elbow pads are for the clumsy."

Isabel demands to know if Eva is calling
her clumsy.

Twin agreement has turned into twin argu-
ment. (Only two letters difference!)

Miraculous moment vanishes as swiftly as
it appeared. One day, Abby Hayes will be
interviewed by news media as eyewitness to
this historic event.

Abby slid her journal back into her gym bag and
moved as far away as possible from her sisters.

"Mom and Dad! Have you ever *tried* Rollerblading?" Alex asked.

"I put on a pair once," their father said. "I stood
up, wobbled in place for thirty seconds, and sat
down again. That was the end of it."

Their mother shook her head in mock dismay.

"What are we going to do with him?"

"Show him, Mom," Abby urged. "Learn to Rollerblade, and then Dad will, too."

"We'll have a Hayes Roller Derby," her father joked as he pulled the minivan into the parking lot. "Maybe we'll sing while we blade."

"Dad!" Isabel and Eva protested in unison.

"It's good to hear you two agree again," their mother commented.

"Even if it's to complain about my bad jokes," their father added. He got out of the car and started to take his bike off the roof rack.

Abby tucked a strand of curly red hair under her helmet. She sat down on a bench and pulled Eva's old Rollerblades out of her gym bag.

They were pale green with plastic buckles. The wheels were scuffed and so were the boots, but she hoped they'd do. She slipped her feet into the boots. Maybe they were a little on the snug side. She tugged at the buckle to lock one Rollerblade. It wouldn't shut.

"Help!" Abby cried. "I can't get it shut!"

"I know how to do it," Eva said. "It's easy."

She kneeled next to Abby and pushed. The buckle clicked into place.

"Will you do the other one?" Abby asked.

"They're sticky sometimes," Eva told her. "You'll get used to it."

"Oh, yeah?" Abby said. That was easy for Eva to say. She could get the best out of any ball, bat, or buckle. Equipment always cooperated with *her*.

Eva rose to her feet. She wore shiny new Rollerblades with an advanced brake system. As Abby watched, her SuperSib sailed down the path with quick, powerful movements. Eva looked like she had been born on Rollerblades!

Isabel tightened her helmet and tried to catch up. She glided after her twin with smooth, easy strokes. She, too, had new Rollerblades. As the oldest, she and Eva never had hand-me-downs.

"We'll meet you back here in a couple of hours!" their mother called after the twins. "Do you have money for a snack?"

"Yes!" Isabel yelled, holding up a five-dollar bill. Then she disappeared down the path.

Abby stared after her sisters. If she had new Rollerblades, would she be as graceful as Isabel and as powerful as Eva?

With a sigh, she fastened her knee, elbow, and wrist pads. They had once belonged to Isabel. At least she had her own helmet! It was purple — her favorite color — with green trim.

A few feet away, their mother did warm-up stretches. Their father, helmeted and gloved, fastened a water bottle to his bike.

He dug in his pockets and pulled out some money. "Here," he said, handling it to Abby. "In case you and Alex get thirsty."

"Sure, Dad." She put the money in her pocket. "Can I keep the change?"

"If it's a few cents, yes. If it's more than a dollar, no." He climbed on his bike. "Ready, everyone?"

Their mother jogged for a moment in place. Alex wobbled over to the path, then found his balance and sped away. Abby followed him. The pavement under her feet felt welcoming. She leaned forward and let herself glide down the path.

The Rollerblades were okay. For now.

"Are you ready to race, Alex?" she called. "I want that ice cream!"

Chapter 2

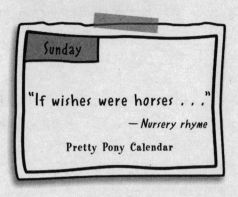

Sunday

"If wishes were horses . . ."
— *Nursery rhyme*

Pretty Pony Calendar

Horses again! Are wishes winged horses or just ordinary ones? If wishes <u>were</u> horses, my room would be full of them. They'd trample all the clothes and books on the floor. They'd eat the candy bars that I've hidden under the bed. They might even nibble on my calendars! I'd have to hide in the attic from all my wishes!

ABBY'S WISH LIST (A small stable's worth)
Pierced ears (Of course)
To be better at something than my Super-

Sibs (Could it ever happen?)

A new pair of Rollerblades — <u>right now</u>!

P.S. I lost the race to Alex. Eva's old Rollerblades wouldn't go fast enough. Then the buckles wouldn't unbuckle, and I had to wait for Eva before I could take them off. Alex won three games of chess in a row! If I had new Rollerblades, NONE of this would have happened.

It's not fair! Eva and Isabel grew out of their old ones. Alex was too small for their castoffs. I'm the only Hayes who didn't get new Rollerblades!

Just because I was born in the middle!

"Look, Abby! There's the poster I want!" Abby's best friend, Jessica, pointed to a picture of the constellations at the back of the poster store. She reached into a pocket of her overalls and pulled out a small zippered purse. "I have just enough money to get it."

"It's very mysterious," Abby said, staring at the starry night of the poster. "If I had it up in my room, I'd want to disappear into it."

Jessica had posters of outer space, the planets, and aliens on the walls of her room. She said that they inspired her to think about the universe and all the unknown discoveries awaiting her. She wanted to be an astronaut when she grew up — or maybe an artist.

"Do you have a Starry Night calendar?" Jessica asked her.

Abby shook her head. She had almost every other kind of calendar. There were seventy-five of them on her walls and on her desk. Posters were too big and too permanent for her. She liked changing the month — and the picture — on her calendars every thirty days. It was magical, like opening windows that had never existed before.

"Poster 691, please," Jessica said to the store clerk.

He searched in a bin and pulled out a cardboard tube. "That'll be twelve ninety-five," he said.

Jessica counted out the money in neatly arranged bills. "There goes my baby-sitting cash." She shrugged. "But I'll earn more tomorrow when I walk Mrs. Odell's dog."

The two girls walked out of the store. Jessica glanced at her watch. "We have another half hour," she said.

"Let's go that way." Abby pointed toward Edie's Earrings. "I want to get presents for Eva and Isabel. Their birthday is coming up soon."

It was a good excuse to look at earrings. They were what Abby and Jessica wanted most. Abby had a pair of gold hoops hidden in her drawer, waiting for the day when her parents would FINALLY let her get her ears pierced.

"Look! Soccer ball earrings!" Jessica touched her earlobes, as if checking to see if holes had miraculously appeared in them.

"They should be required for all players on the Lancaster Elementary soccer team," Abby said. "Then our parents would *have* to say yes to pierced ears!" She pointed to a pair of basketball earrings. "Eva would like those."

"Eva would like the baseballs, too," Jessica pointed out. "She'd like the volleyballs and the lacrosse sticks and the footballs and the ice skates. There are lots of sports earrings!"

Abby rummaged in her pockets and pulled out seven crumpled dollars. It was all that was left of her allowance from the last month. "The basketball earrings are only three dollars," she said. "But then what would I get Isabel?"

"Fingernail polish," Jessica suggested. She pointed to a row of glittery colors.

"She'll love it," Abby said, picking up a bottle of green nail polish with pink, white, and blue sparkles. Isabel was devoted to her fingernails. "I don't think she has any like this."

Abby paid for the earrings and nail polish.

"We've still got fifteen minutes," Jessica said.

Abby sighed. "I'm out of money. I can't even buy a soda or a donut."

"Me, neither."

The two girls began to walk toward the exit where they had arranged to meet Jessica's mother.

Abby stopped and pointed to a striped sleeveless top displayed in the window of a clothing store. "Look, Jessica. It's you!"

"I love it!" Jessica said. "Stripes are my favorite."

"Maybe your mom will get it for you."

Jessica shook her head. "She thinks this store is too expensive."

"Hi, Jessica. Hi, Abby." It was Brianna, one of their classmates from Lancaster Elementary. She was carrying a huge shopping bag. As usual, her dark glossy hair was perfectly cut. She wore a short white strappy dress, edged in blue lace. Her lips shone from the tinted lip gloss she wore — and what was that on her eyes?

"Is Brianna wearing eyeshadow?" Abby whispered. "Or has she been playing in the mud again?"

"Fat chance," her best friend whispered back.

"You're right," Abby murmured. "Even as a toddler, Brianna played only in imported French mud."

"This is the best store in the mall to shop in," Brianna announced. "The manager is a friend of my mother's and lets me come in and buy clothes all by myself. I'm the only fifth-grader in the city with her own charge account. Right, Bethany?"

Brianna's best friend, Bethany, stumbled behind her. She was carrying two huge shopping bags. Her long blond hair was tangled, and her cheeks were flushed. "Brianna, this is heavy," she complained.

"My mother is going to pick us up in an hour, Bethany," Brianna snapped. "Be patient."

She turned back to Abby and Jessica. "Where's Natalie?" she asked. "The three of you are always together."

Natalie had moved to their neighborhood in September. She had quickly become good friends with Abby and Jessica. She was short and thin, and her sweatshirts were always covered with mysterious stains from the chemistry experiments she loved to do. She also loved Harry Potter books, mysteries, and acting.

"She's at drama class," Abby said.

"Which one?" Brianna demanded.

Abby and Jessica glanced at each other. A few months ago, Natalie had won the role of Peter Pan from Brianna and had given an outstanding performance in the play. Brianna hadn't forgotten it.

"It's a workshop given by the city's Youth Arts Council," Jessica said.

Brianna waved her hand dismissively. "I attend private classes taught *only* by professional actors."

"Brianna!" Bethany whined. "I want to sit down."

"All right, all right!" Brianna flipped her dark hair like a model in a television commercial. "Let's go get smoothies at the food court." She waved to Abby and Jessica. "See you in school! Wait until you see my new outfits!"

"Is she a member of the Dress-of-the-Day Club?" Abby asked as soon as Bethany and Brianna were out of earshot. "From the looks of those bags, she bought enough to clothe the entire fifth grade! I wish

I could have just half of her clothes!"

Jessica pulled out her asthma inhaler and took a puff. "I'd buy overalls and T-shirts instead of those dresses she always wears."

"Jessica!" Abby stopped suddenly. "There they are," she said in a hushed voice. She gestured at the display in the sports store window.

"Hockey pucks?" Jessica asked. "Are you thinking of going out for the hockey team, Abby?"

"No, never! Do you think I'm crazy? They practice at six-thirty in the morning. It's the Rollerblades," Abby explained. "And *those* are the ones I've always wanted."

They were dark and shiny, with buckles that surely weren't stiff and resistant. Best of all, they had purple wheels with a swirling, bright design that would flash when they turned. With those Rollerblades, she would fly like a bird. Isabel and Eva would never be able to catch up with her. Alex would never win another race.

"I have to have them," she said to Jessica. "No matter what it takes!"

Chapter 3

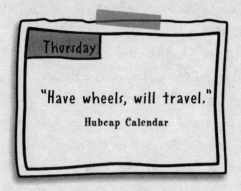

Thursday

"Have wheels, will travel."

Hubcap Calendar

It all depends on what KIND
of wheels! If you have new turquoise
Rollerblades with pink sparkles, speedy
wheels, and high-tech brakes, like Brianna,
you really <u>can</u> travel. You can
skate to school, do fancy turns
and jumps, and
impress the entire class.

If you have your older sister's
cast-off Rollerblades, you poke
along, pretending that you're just
too mature to do those silly
twirls. You try not to trip over

your own feet. If you're lucky, you won't fall on your face in front of your classmates. (I didn't.)

Everyone is skating to school!

There are kids with new Rollerblades, like Meghan, who can barely stand up on them. She has to hold on to fences, trees, and people's hands. Nobody noticed my slow, old-fashioned, boring Rollerblades until I got to school, where I had to ask my friends (Jessica, Natalie) for help to get the buckles undone. Like a five-year-old who can't get her boots off without Mommy.

Mason offered to get a saw from home to cut them off my feet. "Just in case three people can't unfasten one pair of Rollerblades," he said.

Entire fifth grade very amused. Jokes about saws, blowtorches, and high-power lasers for rest of day.

I NEED NEW ROLLERBLADES!!! NOW!!!

How to get new Rollerblades:
1. Parents will suddenly decide to buy them for me. (Fat chance! New Rollerblades

are "too expensive" and Eva's old ones are "good enough.")

2. The perfect birthday present. (Must wait six months.)

3. Rollerblades will arrive on our doorstep with a note saying "Please love me." (Only in fairy tales.)

4. Will win pair in contest. (Which contest, and do they award Rollerblades as prizes?)

5. Get adopted by millionaire. (Only if friends and family visit me at mansion.)

Is there something I've forgotten?

Oh, yeah.

6. Buy them myself.

Math problem: Abby Hayes has $15.53 in her bank account. Each week her loving parents give her $3.00 allowance. If Rollerblades (new, fancy, with purple wheels) cost $60.00 plus 8 percent tax, how many weeks will it take for her to save up the money to buy them?

Answer: Too many! Spring and summer will be over before I have enough money to buy new Rollerblades. I have to figure out how to earn $45.00 – FAST!

Ms. Kantor, the fifth-grade teacher, clapped her hands to get the students' attention.

"Creative writing will begin in just a few minutes!" she announced. "Put away your work, and get out your writing journals."

Abby's journal, blank paper, pencils, and purple pen lay neatly on her desk. She was *always* ready for creative writing class!

Across from her, Tyler and Zach stared at a small electronic screen concealed behind a book.

Abby nudged them. "Hide it!" she warned.

The electronic device disappeared into Tyler's backpack.

"Tyler! Zach!" Ms. Kantor warned. "If I see that again, I'll take it away."

If Ms. Kantor takes away their electronic games, Z and T will shrivel into tiny gray moon men (their true selves).

A few seats behind them, Mason snorted. When Ms. Kantor turned her back, he aimed a paper airplane. It flew down the aisle and landed in front of Brianna.

Oops! Why did Mason fly his airplane to Brianna? She picked it up like it was a disgusting bug and crumpled it into a ball.

"Awwww!" Mason said.

"Class!" Ms. Kantor warned. "Settle down."

Ms. Bunder, the creative writing teacher, entered the classroom. Usually she carried a bag of books and papers. Today, however, her arms were empty.

The fifth-grade girls eyed her outfit enviously. Ms. Bunder wore a short blue dress with dark red embroidery. Garnet earrings dangled from her ears.

"I'll be in the library if you need me," Ms. Kantor said. She shut the door behind her.

"What are we doing today, Ms. Bunder?" Abby called out.

Ms. Bunder looked embarrassed. "I forgot my creative writing folder," she said. "I left it at home."

"Does this mean we skip class?" Tyler asked. "Can we have extra recess instead?"

"No such luck, Tyler!" Ms. Bunder laughed. "I've decided that *you* will help me think of the assignment!"

"Me?" Tyler said. "No way!"

"The whole class is going to think up topics." Ms. Bunder picked up a piece of chalk. "We'll vote on our favorites."

Brianna's hand shot up. "A play about our lives?"

"Starring Brianna, my best friend," Bethany chirped. "Yay, Brianna."

 Brianna <u>should</u> have her own soap opera! <u>Brianna's Life</u> – written, directed, produced, and acted by Brianna. With supporting appearances by Bethany (uncredited).

"Inventing a game?" Zach suggested.

"Does Zach ever say a sentence without the word 'game' in it?" Abby whispered to Natalie.

"Sometimes." Natalie grinned. There were weeks when she spoke of nothing but Harry Potter.

"Any other ideas?" Ms. Bunder wrote on the board with a piece of yellow chalk.

"The Most Disgusting Thing I Ever Did!" yelled Mason.

"He'd have a hard time choosing," Brianna said loudly.

Ms. Bunder ignored her. "I want two or three more suggestions," she said.

Meghan raised her hand. "Pets?" she suggested. "Like writing about our cats?"

If this is our assignment, I will write about a blue-tongued skink!
(Note to self: find out what a blue-tongued skink is!)

"What about something we want really badly?" Abby asked.

Ms. Bunder nodded. "Do you mean a goal or a wish?"

"Rollerblades," Abby said.

"I remember when I wanted a trick bike," Ms. Bunder told the class. "My parents wouldn't buy it because I already had a bicycle. I saved for six months to get that trick bike!" She shook her head. "This is a topic everyone can relate to!"

"I hope it won't take me six months to get new Rollerblades," Abby said to Jessica. "I want them in six days!"

Her friend nodded sympathetically.

"Time to vote!" Ms. Bunder announced. One by one, she read each idea and asked the students to raise their hands for their favorite.

"Meghan's pets and Abby's wishes are tied for first place! You have a choice of what to write about."

"I suppose I'll write about my horse," Brianna sniffed.

Tyler and Zach high-fived each other. "Computer pets!" they yelled in unison.

Natalie gazed dreamily out the window. "I wish I attended Hogwarts," she said. Jessica had already started to write about wanting to explore space and the planets.

Abby took a fresh sheet of paper and wrote her name at the top. With pen in hand and an idea in her brain, she felt as if she could do anything. That was probably how Zach and Tyler felt in front of a computer. Or how her sister Eva felt with a ball in her hands.

When she was writing, it was the best of all possible worlds. Ms. Bunder's class was the cherry on top of the ice-cream sundae.

Chapter 4

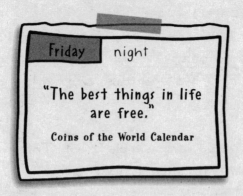

Friday night

"The best things in life
are free."

Coins of the World Calendar

No one in the fifth grade would agree
with that. All of our Best Things cost
money:

Computers, clothes, posters, calendars,
books, bikes, earrings, chemistry sets, soccer
balls, and, OF COURSE, Rollerblades.

Are _any_ Best Things free?

Writing (Must buy pen and notebook.)
Friends (Can't just sit around all the time!

Have to <u>do</u> things together, like eat pizza or go to movies.)

Family (Must be fed, clothed, sheltered, and entertained. This is why parents won't buy me new Rollerblades when old, beat-up ones still fit.)

Okay, okay, try simple Best Things.

Lying in sunshine (Must wear sunblock lotion.)

Swimming in lake (Bathing suits, towels, snacks)

Breathing air (Free for me. But Jessica needs asthma inhaler.)

NOTHING is free anymore!

<u>Abby's Marvelous Money-Making Projects</u>

1. Collected all empty cans and bottles in house. Went to neighbors' houses and asked for more bottles and cans. Put in big plastic bags and lugged to supermarket to redeem.

Work time: 1 hour, 45 minutes

Bottles and cans redeemed: 74

Net profit: $3.70

Amount of money still needed for Rollerblades: $45.00

Supermarket did not give me cash. Got credit slip instead!

Used credit slip to buy candy for consolation.

2. Allowance

Work time: 20 minutes per day

Profit: $3.00

Amount of money still needed for Rollerblades: $42.00

3. Walked along street, looking for money. Natalie told me she found $20.00 in melting snow once. If I find only two $20.00 bills, I will have enough for Rollerblades. Why not?

Work time: 2 hours (approximately)

Profit: $37

Amount of money still needed for Rollerblades: $41.63

CHANGE OF SUBJECT! I'm sick of

thinking about money (though not of imagining self on new Rollerblades with purple wheels).

Hayes Family News, brought to you by the Roving Reporter, Abby Hayes

Tonight, at the Hayes dinner table, birthday party plans for Isabel and Eva were discussed.

No one expected the Terrific Twins to agree on anything, and they didn't.

Eva wanted to attend a college basketball game with her entire basketball team, then go to Paradise Pizza for pizza and ice cream.

Isabel wanted to visit a historical museum with several dozen of her closest friends, then go to a coffeehouse for music and desserts.

Two big parties on the same day! This is a lot of work for Paul and Olivia Hayes.

"Why don't you have one big party at home?" Abby suggested to her older sisters.

(Note to self: Could be professional party consultant and charge $10.00 for brilliant ideas like this one.)

"We could hold it in the backyard," their mother added, with a grateful nod to her red-haired youngest daughter. "The weather will be warm enough."

Eva and Isabel were suddenly on the same side. Neither one wanted a combined party. They both said that outdoor parties were for little kids only. Even when parents offered to invite every ninth-grader in the city, with tents in the backyard and loud-speakers for loud music, SuperSisters still refused.

(Now understand why consultants charge such high fees. Stubborn clients.)

Finally, a compromise was reached. All parties agreed to throw two parties (ha-ha), if Eva and Isabel invited only three friends each.

Parties will be separate and small. Mother will accompany Eva's; Father will tag along at Isabel's.

As for Alex and Abby Hayes . . .

"Mom! I'll baby-sit Alex!" I shouted. "Please!"

"You don't want to go to your sisters'

parties?" Olivia Hayes asked, frowning.

"No!" answered Abby, Alex, Eva, and Isabel all at once.

The Hayes parents seemed disappointed that everyone wanted to go their own way. "Aren't we a family?" they said.

"We'll have a family party," Isabel insisted.

Paul and Olivia Hayes finally agreed to pay Abby twelve dollars for an afternoon of baby-sitting, plus rent videos for her and Alex to watch. Abby will check in with Jessica's mom every hour.

Hooray! Hooray! Hooray! Abby and Alex will not have to tag along at basketball game or (ugh!) historical museum. Abby will also make money for Rollerblades.

The only problem is that Eva and Isabel's birthday is not for another few weeks. Abby Hayes needs new Rollerblades sooner than that!

After this long family discussion, Eva Hayes left for a basketball game.

Isabel Hayes went upstairs to do homework and meditate on her fingernails.

Paul Hayes retired to his home office to finish some urgent work.

Alex Hayes asked Abby to play chess with him, but she had already promised to meet her friends in the park.

LATER

Met most of my classmates in the park. They were all on Rollerblades. Was it an impromptu Rollerblading party?

Or had aliens secretly beamed messages to all of us telling us to meet at 6:30 P.M. by the fountain?

What will the aliens do next? If they want our Rollerblades, they'll need a blow-torch to get mine off! (Mason was right; but I'll never let him know.)

Bethany and Brianna (the B/Bs) were on matching Rollerblades. Brianna swooped, twirled, and spun in circles, in an excellent imitation of a well-dressed spinning top.

Personal cheerleader Bethany followed her everywhere. But when Bethany tripped, Brianna didn't notice. Was busy showing off her jumps.

After Rollerblading around the fountain a couple of times, Zach and Tyler sat on a bench and played electronic games. Zach's mother sent them to the park because they spend too much time in front of a screen.

Natalie appeared with a book under her arm. "Your parents told me you were here," she said to us. "I decided to come to the park. This way I can read <u>and</u> see my friends."

Natalie doesn't have Rollerblades and doesn't want them.

This is a mystery to me. How could anyone NOT want Rollerblades? Her parents are dying to buy them for her.

"Have them buy you Rollerblades and give them to me," I suggested.

We compared feet. Mine were much smaller than hers. Too bad!

Jessica and I skated around for a while, stop-

ping to check in with Natalie and see what
was happening with Harry Potter
and Hermione every now and then.

 We saw Mason sitting on a
baby swing with his little brother.
Looked like he was going to
break it, but he didn't.
"Do you sleep in your
Rollerblades?" he yelled at me
and Jessica.
"YES!" we yelled back.
His baby brother unloaded a fistful of
banana on Mason's head.
"Do you sleep with banana in your
hair?" I called.
He scowled. "Very funny."
Meghan wobbled over on her new
Rollerblades. "I can't stay up," she complained. Her hair was all tangled and sweaty.
Jessica and I each took one of her
arms. We showed her how to move her
feet outward in a skating motion. Finally
she got it! She skated from the fountain to
the benches without falling down.

Felt very proud. Jessica and I high-fived Meghan. Maybe can give Rollerblading lessons for money. (Won't charge Meghan, as she is classmate.)

When it started to get dark, we all went home. All the lights were on in my house, but the door was locked. No one answered when I rang.

Thought quickly. Had aliens abducted my family? Probably fascinated by SuperSib Twindom. Wanted to make Eva and Isabel queens of distant worlds.

Wished one or two aliens had stayed behind to help me take off my Rollerblades.

And why didn't they leave a note?

Dear Abby,

We have taken your family to Mars on our spaceship. Don't worry; we'll return them in a few weeks. To compensate for your loss, we've left $45.00 on the kitchen table. Buy yourself some new Rollerblades.

Your friends,
The Aliens

Would I still want new Rollerblades if my family were floating around in space?

Maybe.

After five minutes, realized that aliens didn't exist. Decided that the Hayes family had overwhelming, sudden urge for ice cream. Maybe they were at the park now, looking for me with a pistachio, strawberry swirl, bittersweet triple cone.

After ten minutes, imaginary ice cream melted into puddle. Decided to skate to Jessica's house and ask her mother what to do. Was just going down sidewalk when entire family drove up in minivan.

"Where were you?" I cried. "Did you forget about me? I've been waiting all alone in the dark!!"

My mother rolled down her window. "Abby! I hoped we would get back before you did. We were at the emergency room. Eva broke her arm!"

Chapter 5

Friday night

"A stitch in time saves
nine."

Knitted Cap Calendar

Eva had 17 stitches on her chin. Do those 17 stitches save 153 later on? (17 x 9 = 153) Eva said 17 was bad enough! She doesn't want any more!

Visiting emergency room is becoming Hayes family hobby. First Alex, now Eva. (At least I wasn't baby-sitting for her, ha-ha.) Will create special category in <u>Hayes Book of World Records</u> for Most Stitches in One Family!

The whole family accompanied Eva into the house. Her right arm was in a sling. She was still wearing her basketball shorts and jersey with number one on the back. Her face had a bandage on it, and she looked angry and upset.

"A player from the other team tripped me!" she kept saying over and over again. "She did it on purpose!"

"You won the game," Isabel said in a soothing tone of voice. "I called Susanna from the hospital to find out."

"Serves them right!" Eva fumed. "They deserved to lose!"

"Take it easy," their father said. "Accidents happen."

"It *wasn't* an accident, Dad! That's what I keep telling you! Why don't you believe me?"

"The ref told me that she fouled you," Paul Hayes said. "He didn't say anything about tripping."

"So he missed it! That doesn't mean it didn't happen!" Eva shouted. "They ought to throw her off the team!"

"Okay, okay, everyone," their mother said. "Eva, sit down and rest. All that yelling is going to hurt when your anesthesia wears off."

"I'll make you some hot chocolate," Isabel offered.

"Thanks," Eva muttered, sinking down into a chair.

"Alex, it's time for bed," their father said. "Okay, Eva? Can we get you something before we disappear?"

"I'm fine," Eva snapped. "Go away and stop fussing over me."

Olivia Hayes rummaged in her briefcase. "I have to look over some papers. I'll be up in Dad's office if you need me."

Eva stared straight ahead. Isabel put a cup of hot chocolate on the table next to her. It had a crown of whipped cream, with shaved chocolate on the top.

"Want one?" Isabel said to Abby, who was eying it enviously.

"Sure." Abby stared at her older sister. She had never seen Isabel so full of sweetness and light.

She searched her brain for something comforting to say to Eva. One of her calendars would have just the right saying, but they were upstairs on the walls of her bedroom.

Don't worry — everything will be okay. Should she say that? No, everything *wasn't* okay.

Cheer up? That was lame.

Time heals all wounds? Better. But *how much* time, Eva might ask. What would Abby reply to that? The doctor had said at least six weeks. Eva had to be very careful not to reinjure her arm or she'd have to have surgery that would require *months* of recuperation. Abby didn't want to remind her sister of the facts. They weren't exactly cheering.

"You know what's the absolute worst?" Eva burst out, as Isabel returned with the second cup of hot chocolate. "I sit out the end of basketball season and ALSO miss softball, lacrosse, swimming, and rowing practice! Even when I'm out of this sling, it'll take me weeks to get back into shape!"

Abby sipped the hot chocolate that Isabel set in front of her. Eva hadn't touched hers.

"That's two months!" Eva fumed. "Two months without sports! All because some idiot tripped me!"

Isabel shook her head sympathetically. "Use the time to read. That's what I would do."

"Of course you would!" Eva snapped. "All you do is read! *You* should have broken your arm instead of me!"

Isabel's fists clenched, and she scowled fiercely at her twin. "Exactly what do you mean by *that*, Eva Hayes?"

Uh-oh. Was another war about to break out? Hadn't the Hayes family had enough excitement for one night?

Abby jumped to her feet. "Wait right here!" she commanded her sisters. She ran upstairs, grabbed a bag from her desk drawer, and rushed back downstairs.

Her two sisters were glowering at each other from opposite sides of the room.

Abby reached into the bag. "Here, Eva. Something for you."

"What is it?" Eva frowned.

"Open it up and see," Abby urged.

Eva glared one last time at Isabel. Then, reluctantly, she took the box that Abby held out to her. With her left hand, she awkwardly pried open the lid and stared at the basketball earrings nestled in cotton.

"Happy birthday three weeks early," Abby said. "If you can't dribble a basketball, at least you can wear them on your ears."

"Thanks," Eva said. She even smiled a little. "That's really sweet of you, Abby."

"I thought you would like them."

Isabel joined her two sisters. "Those are cute!" she exclaimed. "Where did you find them?"

"At Edie's Earrings at the mall." With a sigh of relief, Abby plopped back down in her chair. Her sisters were speaking.

She picked up her cup of hot chocolate. Well, now it was warm chocolate, but it was still good. Especially the whipped cream on top. "They have all kinds of sports earrings," Abby continued. "Baseball, lacrosse, hockey . . ."

"I ought to break my limbs more often." Eva shook her head. "I can't believe I'm joking about this!"

"Maybe you'll get lacrosse earrings next time," Isabel said. "What will you give *me*, Abby, if I break a bone?"

Abby rummaged in the bag. "Fingernail polish," she said, handing Isabel the bottle she had bought at the mall. She hadn't planned to give it to Isabel, but why not? This way, both twins would have their birthday presents at the same time. "Happy three-weeks-early birthday."

"Hey! This is great! I don't have this shade of green!" Isabel said. "And I didn't have to go to the emergency room, either."

"Lucky you," Eva grumbled.

The twins looked at each other, then burst out laughing.

Today I made the world a better place.
Left Eva and Isabel in kinder, gentler

mood than I found them. Prevented War of SuperSisters from wreaking havoc on universe. At least for a few minutes.

(Question: What is "havoc" and why is it "wreaked"? Doesn't sound like English at all. Must be alien language. Is "wreaking havoc" a dance that they do on Saturday nights?)

All it took to restore world peace was a pair of earrings and a bottle of green fingernail polish. Must be sure to share my methods with peace negotiators worldwide. (Could become professional peace consultant and charge big fee — $45.00?)

One problem: Will Eva and Isabel forget that nail polish and earrings are early birthday presents? Will they expect second set of birthday presents? How will I get cash for more presents AND Rollerblades?

Now understand why world peace is such a difficult goal. Too many sacrifices!

Chapter 6

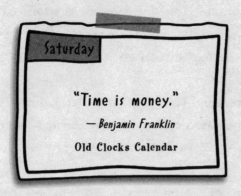

> **"Time is money."**
> — Benjamin Franklin
> Old Clocks Calendar

Saturday

Oh, yeah? I think money is time! With money, I can <u>save</u> time spent Rollerblading with Eva's old beat-up Rollerblades. With money, I will be able to <u>spend</u> time on newer, faster Rollerblades that everyone in the fifth grade will admire!

Earned: $2.00 for washing minivan
Spent: $1.75 on ice cream cone (was hot and hungry after working on van)
Amount closer to goal: $.25
Needed for new Rollerblades: $41.38

* * *

<u>Why</u> can't I save any money?

At least I don't have a broken arm. Or leg. Just a hole in my pocket. Poor Eva! Will she be upset when she sees me on Rollerblades?

She already told me not to worry. "Go ahead and have fun," she said with a sad wave of her arm. "<u>Someone</u> has to."

Number of phone calls to Hayes residence since Eva's accident: 254

Number that were for Eva: 247

Advantages of broken arm: can't cook, load dishwasher, vacuum, take out garbage, scrub bathtub, or do any household chores. Can't make bed in morning, do homework, take tests, or carry 400-pound backpack (just kidding, I think) to school.

Advantages Eva sees in broken arm: none

Size of dark, gloomy cloud hanging over Eva's head: gigantic

Size of dark, gloomy cloud hanging over my head: As big as two twenty-dollar bills. That's smaller than

Eva's because at least I can still Rollerblade!

Worst news of the day: I offered to do chores for Eva in exchange for her allowance ($7.00). Eva says she will get allowance <u>without</u> doing chores because she has perfect excuse. Doesn't need to hire younger sister desperate for money. Boo-hoo!

Best news of the day: Our neighbor, Heather, is going out of town for a week. She wants one of the Hayes girls to take care of her cat, Marshmallow. Eva can't, Isabel won't, but I can and will! I will earn $10.00! Hooray!

Abby opened the window in her room, and a cool breeze ruffled the pages of the calendars on her wall. She had already done her Saturday morning chores, picked up her room, and helped her father and Alex wash the minivan.

Before she met Natalie and Jessica at the park, she had to stop by Heather's apartment for the key and instructions on how to take care of Marshmallow the cat.

Abby put on a light jacket, skipped down the stairs and out the front door of her house.

Half a block away, Heather sat on her front porch, taking notes as she read a thick book. She was a graduate student at the university and spent most of her time studying or writing papers.

"Hey, Abby!" she called. *"¡Hola!"* She put down the pen and ran her fingers through her curly brown hair.

Heather's hair was almost as wild and messy as Abby's. She usually wore it up in a ponytail, but sometimes she let it go untamed and free. She wore blue jeans and heavy sweaters that she knit herself. She traveled often and always brought back delicious chocolate bars and other treats for the Hayes family.

"Did you make that sweater?" Abby asked, pointing to the black speckled wool sweater that Heather wore.

"Of course," she said. "I finished it yesterday. I'm going to wear it on my trip. Do you like it?"

"Yes," Abby said. It looked warm and comfortable. "Was it hard to make?"

"Not really," Heather said. "I can show you how to knit sometime. It's easy!"

"Maybe," Abby said doubtfully. Somehow she imagined that if she tried to knit, the wool would end up in a tangle, and anything she made would either be ten sizes too big or too small.

Heather stood up and stretched. "I wish I could take today off and go hiking in the woods. But I have to get this reading done before I leave for London. Would you like to come in? I'll show you where I keep Marshmallow's food. *¡Andale!* Come on!"

Heather's father was Mexican; her mother was American. She had spoken Spanish and English since she was a baby.

The apartment was dark after the dazzling sunshine outside. Abby blinked her eyes. The living room had a futon, shelves of books, and a computer on a desk. There were piles of CDs on the floor.

"Marshmallow!" Heather called. "Abby's here!"

Marshmallow, a pale, sleek cat wearing a blue collar with a bell, lifted her head and meowed. She perched on the windowsill, watching something on the lawn outside.

"There you are, my little baby," Heather crooned. "Come to Mommy!"

The cat meowed again and swished her tail back and forth. As Heather approached, Marshmallow bounded off the windowsill and disappeared under the futon.

"She's shy," Heather explained. "She'll be friendlier when you feed her. Come into the kitchen. I'll show you where everything is."

Abby followed Heather into the kitchen. There were pots, pans, dried flowers, and strings of garlic hanging on the walls.

"The garlic keeps away the vampires," Heather said with a grin.

"You have vampires?" Abby said nervously. Is this why Heather was paying so much for her to take care of Marshmallow?

"Just a joke!" Heather said. "I bought the garlic at the farmers' market. I have enough for the next two years!"

She opened the refrigerator. "This is where I keep Marshmallow's canned food once it's opened. Give her one-quarter of a can of wet food and a big scoop of dried food every day. Change her water every time you come, and change the litter box at least twice this week."

"Okay," Abby said. It didn't sound too hard — except the part about the litter box. But she guessed she could do that, too. For money for Rollerblades, she'd do almost anything.

Heather dug into her jeans pocket and pulled out a key on a red ribbon. "Here's my extra key," she said. "Always lock up when you leave."

"Yes," Abby said. "I'll remember."

"And don't let Marshmallow out! There's too much traffic in this neighborhood."

"I won't let her out," Abby repeated.

Heather nodded. "I know you're responsible and will take good care of Marshmallow." She reached into her pocket once more and handed Abby five dollars. "Here's half the money in advance. I'll give you the rest when I get back."

"I'll take really good care of Marshmallow," Abby promised.

As if she had heard her name, Marshmallow strolled into the kitchen. She rubbed her head against Abby's leg and purred.

"She likes you!" Heather exclaimed.

Abby leaned over to pet Marshmallow. "We like each other, isn't that right, Marshmallow?"

The cat purred even more loudly.

A few minutes later, Abby was hurrying toward the park and doing arithmetic in her head: $41.38 for Rollerblades, minus ten dollars for taking care of Marshmallow, equaled $31.38. That was a *lot* closer to her goal!

If she had three more jobs like this, she'd be gliding to school on new Rollerblades in a matter of days! No one would make jokes about her needing saws and blowtorches to take them off, either!

"Abby! Abby!" Jessica and Natalie were standing at the entrance of the park, waving wildly at her.

"Guess what?" Natalie yelled. She wore a sweatshirt, jeans, and white sneakers splattered with greens, blues, and yellows. Had the sneakers been worn to art class, or during an experiment? Even Natalie might not know. "I have something exciting to tell you!"

"Me, too!" Abby yelled as she ran toward her friends. She waved the five-dollar bill in the air. "I'm rich!"

Her friends applauded.

Abby put the money back in her pocket. "What's

your good news?" she asked Natalie.

"My parents are taking us to the state park. We're going to rent rowboats, and you and Jessica are invited!"

"I have permission already," Jessica said. "We tried to call you, but Isabel said you were already gone."

"My parents will say yes," Abby said. "My chores are all done. I just have to ask them."

The three friends linked arms and began to walk toward Natalie's house.

Chapter 7

Sunday

"Fate keeps on happening."
— *Anita Loos*

Greek Tragedy Calendar

Does it ever!

Fateful events in my life:

1. Went rowing.
2. Very hungry afterward.
3. Food locked in Natalie's car.
4. Natalie's parents temporarily out of sight.
5. Sandie's Snack Shack open.
6. No one had money but me.

I bought us all slices of pizza and a soda that we shared. Natalie and Jessica offered to pay me back, but I said no. They told me my noble sacrifice would never be forgotten. Would go down in history.

(That _is_ consolation, but would rather have $5.00.)

Spent on friends and self: $4.55

Saved toward Rollerblades: $.45

Found in grass at state park, including two quarters Natalie and Jessica gave me: $.83

Needed for new Rollerblades: $35.35

I am only nickeling and diming toward my goal, when I should be dollaring!

Eva is also in the grip of fateful events.

(Question: Why do fateful events grip? Why don't they pinch, tickle, bump, bruise, and shake? That's what they're doing to Eva!)

Eva has to ask for help for _everything_.

Except breathing. She can still do that.
And talking. Her jaw is sore but that
doesn't stop her. Her stitches come out in a
few days. Then she will talk even more!

Alex offered to design a robot that would
carry her backpack to school, write her papers, and bring her lunch tray to the table.

Eva didn't think Alex could do it. But I
think she underestimates him.

Is Alex a computer in disguise? No, a
computer would never put its clothes on
backward. And computers can be beaten at
chess!

If Alex designs a robot, I will sell it to
students with broken arms and legs. Will
take only a small percentage of profits . . .

P.S. Have finally thought of a Best Thing
in life that is free: whole, unbroken bones!
Broken bones are a Worst Thing — especially
when you're an athlete like Eva. You have
to pay for them, too! I saw the bill on
the kitchen table last night. No wonder my
parents don't want to buy me new
Rollerblades when Eva's still fit me! (For the

price of a broken arm, I could buy <u>dozens</u> of new Rollerblades!)

Tomorrow I start taking care of Marsh-mallow! Five minutes of work a day for five more dollars! I can't believe I'm get-ting paid so much to do so little!

Abby closed her purple notebook and sleepily turned over in bed. It was Sunday morning, and the Hayes house was momentarily quiet. From the smell of cof-fee wafting upstairs, she knew that her father, still in his bathrobe, was in the kitchen reading the Sunday paper. Her mother was out jogging already; the front door had slammed half an hour ago. Eva and Isabel were still asleep — at least she thought they were — and Alex was at the computer. She could hear the faint sounds of electronic battle coming from his bed-room.

On Sunday mornings, Abby liked to relax and gaze at the calendars on her walls. Jessica wanted to visit other planets, but Abby thought that traveling in her imagination was even better. The pictures on her cal-endars transported her to other worlds. She could travel in space and time without leaving her bed.

Today, however, she was going to harness the power of her imagination for new Rollerblades.

Abby climbed out of bed and went to her desk. She ripped a sheet of lined paper from her school notebook and wrote at the top of the page:

<u>Abby's Schemes and Dreams</u>

 Dreams: Rollerblades with purple wheels! Rollerblades with purple wheels! Rollerblades with purple wheels! Rollerblades with purple wheels! Rollerblades with purple wheels! Rollerblades with purple wheels! Rollerblades with purple wheels! Rollerblades with purple wheels!

(Write one million times, until Rollerblades appear in my room.)

Schemes: Taking care of Marshmallow, collecting allowance, and finding stray coins in grass. At this rate, I won't get Rollerblades until middle school!

Need new schemes that will earn lots of money fast!

1.

2.

3.

4.

5.

6. Lemonade stand? With Alex? If he'll help me?

7.

8.

9.

10.

Abby crumpled up the paper and threw it in the wastebasket. She got up and stared at herself in the mirror. Her left cheek had a red mark where she had rested her hand.

"I am going to have a lemonade stand," she said to her reflection, trying to drum up enthusiasm. A lemonade stand was a second-grade idea, but Abby was desperate. It was her only moneymaking scheme! The power of her imagination had deposited one puny thought in her mind and no more.

She opened her desk drawers and found poster board and markers.

ABBY'S LIVELY LEMONADE, she wrote in bubble letters. She drew a picture of a cup in all four corners, wrote "$ .50 ONLY!" Then she threw on her bathrobe and went downstairs to the kitchen.

"Please, please, *please*, Alex!" Abby begged. "Won't you help me with the lemonade stand? It's so boring to sit out there by myself!"

"I want to play on the computer." Alex sat at the kitchen table eating a muffin with jam. He wore a flannel shirt and pajama bottoms, with two different slippers. A plastic snake dangled from his neck.

"I'm trying to earn money for Rollerblades!" Abby said. "Please? I'll let you make change."

Alex scratched his nose. "The whole time?"

"Of course!" He'd be better at making change than she would, anyway.

"Okay," her brother said. "But you have to play chess with me. Two games for every dollar you earn."

Abby groaned. Sometimes she wished her little brother wasn't so quick. Weren't twin geniuses enough for the Hayes family? "Oh, all right! Two games for every dollar I earn!"

"Shake, partner." Alex stuck out a jam-covered hand. "Are we making pink lemonade? That's my favorite."

"Pink and yellow." The supplies — pitchers, paper cups, and frozen lemonade — had been donated by her family. The stand would be pure profit.

Her father wandered into the kitchen and peered at Abby's sign. "A lemonade stand. How enterprising. Reserve a glass for me."

"Has anyone seen Isabel or Eva?" their mother asked. She was wearing jogging shorts and had her hair tied back with a ponytail holder.

"Isabel went off early to study at the library," their father said. "Eva's still sleeping."

"No, I'm not," a grouchy voice said from the doorway.

It was Eva. Her hair was tangled and messy, and she was still in her pajamas.

"Where's Isabel?" Eva demanded as her family stared at her. "I can't get this stupid pajama top off without her! My hair is a mess, and I can't brush it! I can't even wash my face by myself!" Then she burst into tears.

Chapter 8

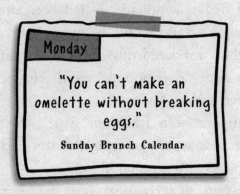

Monday

"You can't make an omelette without breaking eggs."

Sunday Brunch Calendar

What do broken arms make? Not something good, like an omelette. They make a very unhappy sister.

Offered glass of lemonade to Eva for free. (Very generous of me, but hated to see a sister in pain.) While she was drinking it, she spilled some on her pajamas.

In comforting, motherly voice, Mom said, "You'll learn to use your left hand in no time at all."

This made Eva cry even more. Then Alex started crying. Mom looked like she was going to cry, too. Dad kept opening his mouth and then closing it.

"I want Isabel!" Eva sobbed.

Hayes family cry fest was spreading. If I didn't do something fast, I was going to start crying, too.

"I'll get Isabel from the library!" I yelled.

Put down pitcher of lemonade and rushed out door.

Eva still crying when Isabel and I got home. (Don't people run out of tears? Question to pose to scientist. SuperSib will make <u>Hayes Book of World Records</u> for Super-Sob. Will not mention to her until her arm is completely healed.)

Wondered if Isabel would start crying, too. But instead, she put her arm around Eva and led her upstairs.

Are these my sisters? Or astonishing cases of spirit possession?

Half an hour later, they came

back downstairs. Eva was washed, brushed, and dressed. Isabel helped her eat breakfast, and they whispered and talked together.

Hayes family flabbergasted by twin trans-formation. Saw mother and father exchange worried looks. Alex ran to his room. Had to promise him three extra chess games to coax him out to lemonade stand.

Eva sat on front steps and watched us. "Want to help?" I asked her. "No!" she snapped.

First customers arrived a minute later. Bethany and her mom stopped on their way to gymnastics prac-tice. Both drank glasses of lemonade. (Bethany didn't say "Yay, Brianna" once. Too thirsty?)

When they left, Eva said she was sorry for snapping at me. With her left hand, she reached in her pocket and pulled out a dollar bill. "Will you pour me a glass of lemonade?"

"It's free," I said. "Family discount."

Eva drank the lemonade that Alex handed her. She left the dollar bill on the table.

"For your Rollerblading fund," she said. "If you want, I'll come out later and relieve you. If I don't cry into the lemonade and scare away all your customers."

"Thanks, Sis," I stammered.

All-powerful SuperSib reduced to manning lemonade stand? The thought saddened me.

Was also amazed by sister's personality change. She gave me a dollar! She offered to help!

Later:

Earned at lemonade stand: $9.50 (Wow! Great!)

Minutes Eva worked at lemonade stand: 10 (long enough for me and Alex to eat peanut butter sandwiches)

Chess games owed to Alex: 22 (Uh-oh. Maybe he will go Rollerblading with me instead?)

Needed for Rollerblades: $25.85 (getting closer!)

It was Monday morning. Abby slid her purple notebook into her backpack, then took Heather's key from her drawer and tied it to a loop on her jeans. She pulled on a hooded sweatshirt, then glanced at her face in the mirror.

Same face as always. Why couldn't she wake up one morning and look like a planet? Or a calendar? Or even a marigold?

"It would be nice if our faces surprised us once in a while," she said out loud to no one in particular. She picked up her backpack and went downstairs to get breakfast.

"You're up early," her mother said. She was dressed in a pale blue suit with a cream-colored silk blouse and was already on the phone.

"I'm on hold," she said, giving Abby a kiss. "It's not my favorite way to start the day."

"I'm going to feed Marshmallow before school," Abby told her mother. "Then I'll check on her on my way home."

"That's just won — " Her mother switched her attention back to the phone. "Hello? Yes, this is Olivia Hayes."

Abby poured herself a bowl of granola. It was her favorite kind — the one with almonds and raisins and honey, and, best of all, tiny dried raspberries. She sat down at the table and pulled the comics section from the newspaper.

"Can I read them, too?" It was Alex in pajamas and a long fleece hat.

"Why are you wearing a hat?" Abby asked. She pushed the comics toward him.

"My head was cold." He pushed the hat back on his forehead and immediately became absorbed in his favorite comic strip.

Abby looked at the front page of the newspaper. It was upside down; she tried to see if she could read the headlines that way. ˙ ˙ ˙ ɟO N∀Ɔ SANIℲ ⅄Oᗺ

Spiders? Gold coins? Worms? Abby never found out what was inside the can. Her sisters arrived in the kitchen.

"Hello, everyone," Isabel sang out. She was carrying two backpacks — her own and Eva's. Her skirt was long, silky, and sizzling orange. Her T-shirt was short, black, and ribbed. Her eyes were outlined in black pencil, and half a dozen silver rings adorned her fingers.

Eva was right behind her. Instead of wearing her usual neat khaki pants and button-down shirt, she was in sweatpants and a T-shirt. Her hair was in a ponytail, and she — or Isabel — had put on lipstick and the basketball earrings that Abby had given her.

Isabel waved orange-painted fingernails in the air. "Eva dressed herself today," she announced like a proud mother. "Isn't that great?"

Olivia Hayes hung up the phone.

"Mom!" Eva said in a low voice. "I don't want to go to school with a broken arm! Can I stay home?"

"For the next six weeks?" her mother said. "I don't think so!"

"I'll need help. Isabel isn't in any of my classes!"

"Ask your friends," her mother said.

"No!" Eva cried. "*No!*"

Olivia Hayes sighed. "You're going to have to get used to this, Eva. Your broken arm isn't going away. I've written a note to the school nurse. If you have any problems, you can talk to her."

Abby got up from the table. A broken arm wasn't any fun. Still, there *were* advantages. This weekend, Eva had watched hours of television and no one told her to shut it off. She was practically a princess in the Hayes family now.

And Isabel was acting like her knight in shining armor.

As Eva and her mother continued arguing, Abby quietly slipped out the door. No one seemed to notice.

In the hallway, she bent down to tighten her laces. She wasn't going to Rollerblade today; it was supposed to rain and that wouldn't be good for the wheels. The wheels were bad enough already!

"Heading out early?" It was her father, in jeans and a denim shirt. There was a pencil stuck behind his ear, and he was wearing his favorite leather slippers.

"I'm taking care of Heather's cat," Abby told him, showing him the key on the red ribbon. "She's paying me ten dollars."

"That's great!" He gave her a hug, then fished in his pocket and handed her a five-dollar bill. "A small contribution for your Rollerblade fund."

"Wow! Thanks, Dad! You mean it?"

"Hard work and enterprise should be rewarded." Her father put his finger to his lips. "Don't tell your sisters."

"I won't!" She gave her dad a big hug and goodbye kiss and went out the door.

Abby ran down the sidewalk to Heather's apartment. When she least expected it, her father often did something nice for her. This was like money falling from the sky — except she didn't have to worry about who had dropped it and how to return it.

She would do something nice for *him*. Maybe she'd buy him an Internet calendar with funny quotes to cheer him up when his programs crashed — after she had her new Rollerblades, of course. She needed only twenty dollars and eighty-five cents more! The Rollerblades were practically hers!

At Heather's door, she pulled out the key and inserted it into the lock. Marshmallow was meowing loudly behind the door.

"Here I am, Marshmallow!" Abby sang. "I'm going to feed you delicious cat food!"

She turned the key and opened the door.

A pale, furry shape shot past her like a blur. Marshmallow streaked across the porch and disappeared down the street.

Chapter 9

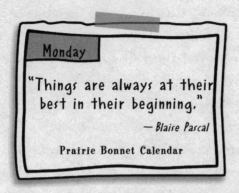

Monday

"Things are always at their best in their beginning."

— *Blaise Pascal*

Prairie Bonnet Calendar

Why are things <u>always</u> best in the beginning? Why not usually, sometimes, occasionally, or NEVER?

Marshmallow escaped at the beginning of my job. If that's the best part, I'm in <u>deep</u> trouble!

Number of times I called Marshmallow: 10,000,000,000,000,000,000,000,002

Places I searched: everywhere in the neighborhood

Marshmallow sightings: 0

My despair: infinite

* * *

Wanted to spend the day looking for
Marshmallow, but had to go to school. Ar-
rived late. Didn't have chance to confide in
Jessica or Natalie — or ask their advice.

News flash!
Marshmallow is on the loose.
The fluffy pale-beige cat zoomed
out between Abby Hayes's legs
when she went to feed her on
Monday morning. Abby
searched frantically but did
not find her.

Marshmallow is the color of a lightly
toasted you-know-what and wears a blue
leather collar around her neck with a little
bell. She isn't allowed to go outside and
doesn't know the dangers that await her.
Speeding cars, bullies, and dogs are not
part of Marshmallow's world. She's a
sweet, loving cat who's never been away
from home and is probably lost and con-
fused. What if she accidentally gets locked
up in a garage or basement? What if she

gets picked up and sent to an animal shelter? <u>How will I ever find her?</u>

Percentage of school time spent worrying about cat: 99.9%

Concentration on schoolwork: less than zero

Number of times Ms. Kantor said, "Abby Hayes! Pay attention!" 44

Math problems missed on quiz: 18 out of 23

Worried looks from Jessica: a lot

Solutions:

1. Give Heather all the money I've saved for Rollerblades to buy a new cat.

<u>A cat isn't a pair of earrings, a calendar, or Rollerblades. You can't go to the store and pick up a substitute. Marshmallow is irreplaceable!!!</u>

2.

3.

4.

5.

6. Leave town, have plastic surgery, and

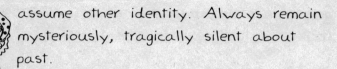

assume other identity. Always remain mysteriously, tragically silent about past.

<u>NOOOOOOOOOO</u>!!!!!! I don't want to leave my family and friends and Ms. Bunder's writing class!!!

Curly red hair a dead giveaway, anyway. Impossible to dye, tame, or hide. Everyone will recognize me. Can't pretend to be anyone other than Abby Hayes.

What should I do? I am at the end of my rope!!!! (Why a rope? Why not a ribbon or a string or a clothesline?)

Okay, I am at the end of my clothesline!!! Help! Help! Help!

Must have said the words out loud, because Ms. Kantor came up to my desk and asked me what was wrong.

"You've been distracted all morning, Abby," she said. "Maybe it will help to tell another person the problem."

I blurted out the story of Marshmallow.

Ms. Kantor nodded, as if she understood. "Don't worry," she said. "Cats are very smart creatures. She'll come home when she's hungry."

"What if she doesn't?" I wailed.

"I have an idea," she said.

Ms. Kantor went to the board. She asked the class to return to their seats and announced that we were going to do a fifteen-minute creative problem-solving exercise together.

Then she told me to stand up and explain the problem.

"Does anyone have an idea of how to get Marshmallow back home?" Ms. Kantor asked.

Dozens of hands shot into the air at once. The great minds of Ms. Kantor's fifth grade were at work. Here is what they came up with:

1. Do an electronic scan of neighborhood (the Game Boy gamies, Tyler and Zach).

2. Buy expensive gourmet cat food, open it on the porch, and wait for cat to appear (Brianna <u>would</u> suggest the Cat's Meow cat food! It costs more than a steak dinner!).

3. Organize search party of friends (Jessica, always helpful).

4. Invent a cat-tracking powder (Natalie offered to concoct one).

5. Post a reward (Mason suggested $100.00. I would want to win it myself!).

6. Buy a special toy that will tempt it home (Bethany says this works for her hamster, Blondie).

Having great minds think about my problem made me feel <u>MUCH</u> better.

Yay, Ms. Kantor! Thanks for having classmates think up solutions.

Results:

– Now have search party. Jessica, Natalie, Bethany, Tyler, Zach, Meghan, and Mason offered to help me look for Marshmallow after school.

Brianna wanted to help, too, but has dance lessons, voice lessons, and acting lessons today. (Wonder if she also has lesson lessons?)

– Have bravely decided to purchase Cat's Meow cat food and toys to lure Marshmallow home, even if they cost lots of money.

– Offered $5.00 reward. Mason very excited. He is saving for a hockey stick and puck.

– Ms. Kantor told me that if I don't find Marshmallow, she will help me talk to Heather about it.

Do not feel so alone. Have friends and teacher on my side.

Ms. Kantor said it was probably not my fault that Marshmallow escaped. Couldn't have been predicted. No one warned me that cat was a professional runner, probably famous in cat world for stunning bursts of speed.

Will put cat in <u>Hayes Book of World Records</u> for Fastest Disappearing Act by Feline.

Did Marshmallow break the sound barrier as she zipped past me?

Chapter 10

Monday still

"A friend may well be reckoned the masterpiece of nature."
— Ralph Waldo Emerson
April Showers Calendar

There are a lot of masterpieces in our neighborhood! (So many that we could open a friendship museum.)

Bethany found Marshmallow!!!
Hidden talents of Brianna's best buddy uncovered. She can wiggle a cat toy and make cat noises better than anyone in the fifth grade. Within minutes, a meowing Marshmallow ran right up to her. Bethany picked

her up and brought her into Heather's apartment.

<u>Yay, Bethany!</u> (Repeat cheer a few thousand times.)

Mason disappointed he did not win reward.

Natalie disappointed that she didn't have chance to invent cat-tracking powder that would make her world famous.

Jessica disappointed that search party did not get a chance to go door-to-door.

But EVERYONE was happy that we found Marshmallow.

Amount needed for Rollerblades <u>before</u> Marshmallow escaped: $20.85

Amount needed for Rollerblades <u>after</u> Marshmallow escaped: $26.32

Expenses: Cat's Meow cat food, toys, treats

Bethany refused reward. She loves ani-

mals and wanted to make sure that
Marshmallow was safe. Yay, Bethany!! Yay,
Bethany!! Yay, Bethany!!

Abby shut the cupboard doors and faced the friends
sitting around her kitchen table.

"I wanted to give you marshmallows," she cried,
holding out empty hands. "But they're all gone!"

"Cookies are okay," Mason said, helping himself
to half a dozen at once.

The search party had come to her house for a
snack party.

"Cookies are great," Tyler and Zach echoed, grab-
bing half the plate. They were doing their best to
keep up with Mason.

What was it with boys, anyway? They ate everything in sight! Bethany didn't seem to mind. She giggled every time she caught Tyler's eye.

"When are you going to visit my hamster, Tyler?"
she asked.

"Mmmff," Tyler said. His mouth was full.

Bethany giggled again.

"Anyone want lemonade?" Abby asked, holding
up the pitcher.

"Me!" Zach said. He kept looking over at Natalie,

who sat with her arms folded around her knees. She was humming a song.

"That's a nice song," he said. "I like your sneakers, too."

Natalie wiggled her toes. "My mother wanted me to buy black sneakers, but I said no."

"I agree." Zach held out his glass for Abby to fill.

"Do you want some?" Abby asked Natalie and Meghan. This hostess stuff was a lot of work! She wanted to sit down and talk to her friends but had to make sure they had food and drink. She hoped they were enjoying themselves. She hoped the boys wouldn't eat *all* the cookies.

Natalie shook her head; Meghan nodded yes.

As Abby was pouring the last of the lemonade, Alex wandered into the kitchen. "Hi," he said. His hair looked particularly electrified today. "I programmed a new robot," he announced.

He wandered out again.

Mason laughed. "My baby brother will be doing that in a year or two," he said.

"Inventing a banana-smearing robot?" Abby retorted.

"Sure," Mason said, stuffing another three or four cookies into his mouth.

"I have three little sisters," Bethany sighed. "Not one of them can program robots." She stood up. "I have to go. My hamster is hungry."

"Thanks for helping with Marshmallow, Bethany!" Abby said for the millionth time. "You were great!"

Bethany smiled. "Anytime."

"I have to go, too," Jessica said. "My mother said to be home by five."

Suddenly, everyone was leaving. The party was over. In what seemed like an instant, Abby's classmates had disappeared, leaving plates, cups, and a lot of cookie crumbs behind.

How exciting was today on a scale from 1 to 10?

Probably an 18. (The scale exploded from too much excitement.)

Am amazed that brain did not explode, too. Is still spinning like a merry-go-round. Can't think straight. Can only think crooked, in whirling circles, or upside down.

Lost and found Marshmallow, discovered unknown Bethany, and threw impromptu party at house . . .

What next???
  Uh-oh! Should not have written those
words. Hear car doors slamming. Loud
laughter and screams. Who is it? What is
. . . Doorbell! Must go!!

Abby opened the front door. Her sister Eva stood
on the porch, flanked by half a dozen basketball players. One carried her backpack, another had
her gym bag, and someone else held a giant teddy
bear.

"See you tomorrow, Captain," they said, giving
Eva a mock salute. They put down the backpack and
gym bag, handed her the teddy bear, and ran back to
the van that waited for them.

"Good-bye!" Eva yelled. "Thanks!"

"Help me carry my stuff in, little sis, okay?" Eva
beamed at Abby.

"Okay, big sis," Abby said, picking up the bags
and darting quick looks at her older sister. Was this
the same person who had been sobbing helplessly
just this morning?

"My friends are the greatest!" Eva cried. "They
formed a tag team and assigned someone to help me

every minute of the day. They carried my books, bought me lunch, and helped with my assignments."

Eva smiled broadly. "I even wrote a few words with my left hand."

Paul Hayes emerged from his office. "I knew you'd be okay, Eva, once you got to school."

"Guess what, Dad? I'm going to be assistant coach. The softball *and* swimming coaches both asked me to help out with practices until my arm is healed. *I'm still number one!*" She punched the air with her strong arm. "And I'm in charge of fund-raising for the team!"

Eva different person from the one who left house this morning. That one tearful and angry. This one beaming and confident.

A mystery of universe, along with pyramids and Bermuda Triangle. Science cannot explain. Rational minds stumped.

Does Eva have a computer chip inside her that Alex reprogrammed?

Did she have a brain swipe? (What *is* a brain swipe? Sounds like a supermarket transaction. Did Eva buy hers on the way to school?) Left-handed writing did it all? She changed her hand *and* her mood?

Eva yanked a pile of tickets from her left-hand pocket. "Anyone want to buy a raffle ticket for the softball team? Only a dollar each! Dad? Abby? One of the prizes is a fifty-dollar gift certificate good at any store in the mall."

"I'll take twelve," their father said. "My lucky number."

Abby shut her journal. She dug three dollar bills from her pocket. "Give me three," she said.

Maybe this was her chance to make up her losses. With a fifty-dollar gift certificate, she'd have more than enough to buy the Rollerblades with purple wheels. But if she didn't win, she'd need twenty-nine dollars and thirty-two cents more!

The front door slammed. Isabel came into the living room. "Hi, everyone. Guess who won the high school civics debate and a seventy-five dollar award?"

"Congratulations," their father said. "Good news is everywhere."

Abby frowned. Why couldn't she win awards like Isabel? Or sell tickets like Eva? Maybe she should have a Rollerblade raffle. What would she give as prizes? Last year's calendars? No one else would want them!

"Want to buy a raffle ticket?" Eva asked her twin. "Support a great cause — our softball team."

"I have better plans for my money," Isabel said.

"Rollerblades?" Abby said hopefully. "For me?"

"Sorry to disappoint you," her sister said. "I'm buying a giant dictionary."

"Dictionary!" Eva cried. "Why waste your money? You're already a walking dictionary."

"For your information, Eva Hayes, knowledge is infinite. It can always be expanded."

"So?"

"I'm not wasting my money on a dumb game!" Isabel snapped.

The twins' eyes glared, their fists clenched, and their jaws jutted out angrily as both switched into battle mode.

"If you two are fighting again, Eva must feel better." Their father shook his head. "I don't know whether to laugh or to cry."

Abby grabbed her journal and ran upstairs. She didn't want to get caught in the crossfire.

Despair! Doom! Discouragement!
Still $30 to go.
Last week, Ms. Kantor read us a book
of Greek myths. My life is like a Greek
tragedy. Can't move forward without slipping
back.

Am I Tantalus trying to pick
a fruit that is always out of
my reach? Or Atlas with the
world on my shoulders? (All I
want is Rollerblades on my feet!)
There is an ancient curse on the
Hayes family! When a red-haired
middle child tries to scrape together a few
pennies for a pair of Rollerblades, the
money mysteriously evaporates into thin air.
(Question: Why not into thick air? Or
chubby air? Or air with lots of pockets?)

When will the curse be lifted? Will Abby
Hayes be the one to finally break the terrible . . .

Interruption! Two raffle tickets just fell
from pages of journal. Now have five total,
even though I only paid for three. Did SuperSis Eva slip extras to me?

She has been behaving very oddly since she broke her arm. Has broken bone affected her brain?

Maybe she gave me a winning ticket!!

Note to self: Check old family diaries in attic. Find where it is written that a broken-armed twin will help a red-haired middle child to lift the Hayes family curse!

Chapter 11

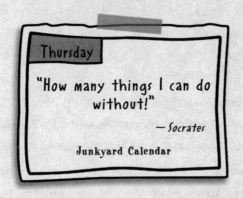

Thursday

"How many things I can do without!"

— Socrates

Junkyard Calendar

How many things I <u>can't</u> do without!
Like Rollerblades with purple wheels! I
need them, I really do!
   Or do I?

   Money needed: $29.32
   Earned: nothing (a tragedy)
   Spent: nothing (a miracle)

   Number of escape attempts by Marshmallow so far this week: 7 (Is she Houdini of
cat world?)

Number of successful escape attempts: 0 (Ha! Ha! Ha!)

Chess games still owed to Alex: 15 (Aaaaaah!)

Marshmallow money spent already. No ideas for earning more. Shall I admit defeat with less than $30 to go?

Eva's old Rollerblades <u>are</u> good enough. Maybe. (Must find secret place to take off. Will crowbar really help with stiff buckles?)

Money runs through my hands like sand. I wish I had as many dollars as grains of sand in a bucket.

How do adults save hundreds of thousands of dollars for cars and houses? Brain transplants? Gene mutations? Vitamin pills?

I do not need new Rollerblades. I do not need new Rollerblades. I do not need new Rollerblades. I do not need new

Rollerblades. I do not need new Rollerblades. I do not need Rollerblades. I do not need new Rollerblades. I do not need new Rollerblades —

Is brainwashing taking effect yet?

I do not need new Rollerblades. I do not need new Rollerblades. I do not need new Rollerblades. I do not need new Rollerblades. I do not need new Rollerblades. I do not need new Rollerblades.

I WANT THEM!!!! I WANT THEM!!!! I WANT THEM!!!! N-O-W!!!!

"Abby, will you help tie my sneakers?" Eva asked. She poked her head in Abby's room. "I can't get them with one hand. Isabel left early. On purpose, I think." She grimaced and adjusted her sling.

Abby picked up her math homework and folded it in two. "How much will you pay me?"

"You charge to tie sneakers? With my broken

arm?" Eva said incredulously. "Is money all you think about?"

"Yes," Abby said. Aside from writing in her journal, seeing her friends, and doing her schoolwork, money — or Rollerblades — WAS all she thought about.

Eva shook her head. "Just tie the sneakers, okay? It's bad enough getting dressed by myself."

"Oh, all right." Abby knelt down and pulled the laces tight.

"Double knot them." Eva sighed impatiently. "I hate having someone tie my shoes in the morning. It's like being four years old again."

"Does that mean I'm your mother?" Abby asked.

Eva combed one hand through her hair. "I don't think so. When you're done with my sneakers, put my hair in a ponytail, okay?"

Abby tied the last knot in Eva's sneakers and stood up. She didn't mind helping out — at least not too much — but she wished Eva wouldn't give orders quite so firmly.

"Please," Eva added, as an afterthought.

"Okay," Abby said. She picked up the hairbrush. "Can I give you lots of braids? I did it for Jessica last week!"

"One plain ponytail is all I want," Eva grumbled. "Save the fancy stuff for Isabel when she breaks *her* arm."

"All right, Captain." Abby began to brush her hair. It was easier than she expected. Her older sister didn't have Abby's wild tangles and snarls. Her hair was straight and thick. It was straightforward, plain-spoken, no-nonsense hair. It was just like Eva. Did people have hair that matched their personalities?

"What's wrong with my old Rollerblades?" Eva asked suddenly. "Why do you want another pair so badly?"

"They're pokey, they have bad brakes, and I can't unbuckle them."

"Too bad I can't lend you my new ones. I sure won't be using them for a while."

"They're too big," Abby said. She was starting to feel like Goldilocks. Or was it the three bears? The Rollerblades were too big, too slow, too expensive, too old. Would she ever get a pair that was just right?

Abby stood back and surveyed Eva's ponytail. It looked pretty good. It wasn't sticking out to one side or the other. "I still need thirty dollars before I can buy myself a new pair." She sighed. "I'm never going to get it. At least not until Rollerblading season is over."

"Are you sure? Aren't you baby-sitting for Alex on my birthday?"

"That's still weeks away!" Abby cried. "I want them now, and I need to earn money to buy them."

Eva frowned. "It shouldn't be hard."

"It *is*!" Abby said. "I make little bits of money and then spend it. I need it all at once in a big lump!"

Eva fished in her left-hand pocket and pulled out a lipstick. "Will you put this on me, Abby?" she asked. "Carefully! I don't want it all over my face."

Abby swiveled the lipstick out of its tube. It was pale pink and smelled faintly of perfume. She drew it lightly over her sister's lips. "Can I try it sometime?"

"You're too young." Eva studied Abby's face for a moment. "But I have an idea."

"For lipstick?" Abby asked hopefully.

"No!" Eva said. "I know how you can make money. Have a garage sale!"

"A garage sale?" Abby had seen plenty of them. Card tables heaped with old, worn-out clothes, ratty stuffed toys, and scuffed shoes. "How much would I make? Fifty cents?"

"Don't laugh," her older sister said. "The garage sale is the swimming team's most successful fundraiser. Last year we raised more than nine hundred dollars. Abby, you're *guaranteed* to earn thirty dollars in the first hour. A garage sale is the answer."

"Yes!!!" Abby cried. "You're right!" She threw her arms around her older sister.

"Don't break my arm again!" Eva winced. "Next time I have to have surgery, and recovery time is a *lot* longer than six weeks." She clumsily patted Abby on the back. "I hope you make the money you need."

Abby stepped back. "You're the greatest, Eva. I'll tie your shoelaces every morning until your sling comes off. For free!"

Eva glanced at her face in the mirror. "There's an offer I can't refuse," she said. "I have to finish getting ready for school now. No one better bump into me in the halls today." She clenched her left fist. "I might just bump back."

When her sister had gone back to her room, Abby sat down on her bed with her journal.

Who says Isabel is Brain of Hayes family? Eva has brilliant brainstorms, too!

(Next Isabel will win a cross-country race. Ha-ha. Will she be wearing her platform sandals to do it?)

Fact #1:

If I hadn't tied her sneakers, put on lipstick, and done her hair, Eva wouldn't have thought of wonderful, easy, complete solution to my problems.

Fact #2:

If Eva hadn't fought with Isabel, she wouldn't have asked me to help her.

Facts #3, 4, and 5:

If Eva hadn't broken her arm, she wouldn't have needed any help. She would have left the house very early for sports practice. I wouldn't have seen her until late tonight.

Conclusion, sort of:

Am I saying that I'm glad Eva broke her arm and fought with Isabel? Sort of, but not exactly. I'm glad that we had a chance to talk.

P.S. Has Eva ended the Hayes family curse? I knew she would!

Chapter 12

Little things I have collected for garage sale tomorrow:

Dented miniature cars (Alex)
Used golf balls (Eva)
5 bottles of half-used nail polish (Isabel)
Box of outdated computer manuals (Dad)
Faded silk flowers (Mom)
Broken crayons, erasers, rulers (me)

Will people pay money for this stuff?
<u>Why?</u>

* * *

Priced everything. Won't make more than a few dollars even if everything sells. Need big things to make money. Or a LOT more little things!

"Here, Marshmallow!" Abby called as she unlocked Heather's door and shut it behind her.

Marshmallow bounded off the couch and ran over to Abby, meowing loudly.

"Yes, I know," Abby crooned, kneeling down to pet the cat. "You're hungry. And I have a can of Salmon Delight for you."

Marshmallow purred and rubbed her head against Abby's ankle. Her tail swished back and forth.

Abby went into the kitchen, refilled the water dish, then set it down.

She opened the refrigerator and took out a can of cat food. Carefully she spooned out the amount that Heather had showed her into Marshmallow's dish.

"Here you go," Abby said. She rinsed off the spoon and put it in the dish drain, then petted Marshmallow for a few more minutes.

She got up and tiptoed toward the door. Yesterday Marshmallow had made a mad dash for the door just as Abby was leaving. She hoped it wouldn't happen again today. The cat looked like a marshmallow, but she ran like a locomotive. Abby could barely keep ahead of her.

In an instant, Marshmallow was at her side, meowing insistently.

"I can't let you out," Abby scolded. "You might get hit by a car." She retraced her steps to the kitchen, opened the refrigerator again, and spooned an extra bit of Salmon Delight into Marshmallow's food dish. The cat sniffed it, then eagerly began to gobble it down.

Abby sped to the door. She closed it behind her and turned the key triumphantly in the lock. Bribery worked! Hooray!

"Cat 1, Human 8," she said, sitting on the front steps and putting on her Rollerblades.

She didn't want to think of the score between her and the Rollerblades. It was probably Rollerblades 57, Human 0.

The buckles were sticking today as usual — or maybe worse than usual. Abby pushed on them as hard as she could, but they wouldn't lock. Now what was she supposed to do? She and Jessica were going to Rollerblade after school!

With a sigh, she took them off and put her sneakers back on. She'd have to carry them to school. If she didn't make enough money tomorrow at the garage sale to buy a new pair, she was going to do something desperate, like take out a loan at the bank.

Did they give bank loans for thirty dollars to kids? They'd probably charge her thirty dollars just to borrow the money!

Abby shouldered her backpack and headed toward school.

She had to find more things to sell. Her gold hoop earrings? No, never! Her shell collection? No one else would want it. Her clothes? Her parents had bought them for her.

There were stacks of boxes in the attic crawl space. Maybe her mother would let her go through them. She'd ask after school. Abby would probably sneeze herself to death bringing the dusty boxes downstairs, but she might find enough sellable objects to make the thirty dollars she needed.

"Guess what?" Natalie said as Abby put down her backpack and Rollerblades in the coatroom. "Ms. Bunder is here!"

"She is?" Abby cried. "Where?"

"In the library, talking to Ms. Yang." Natalie

pulled a battered book from her knapsack. "I thought you might like to know."

"Thanks!" Abby said. She rushed out of the coatroom, almost bumping into Brianna.

Brianna was in the middle of a group of fifthgraders, blocking the way to the door.

"My grandmother won the citywide checkers tournament," she boasted. "She beat a television news reporter half her age."

"Wow," Meghan said.

"Excuse me!" Abby tried to push her way through.

"Grandma Checkers is your grandmother?" Zach asked. "I saw her on television last night."

"She's my grandmother," Brianna said, flipping her hair. "But we don't call her by that silly name. She's Grandma Claudia."

"Yay, Brianna," Bethany said. She was standing next to her best friend, holding her books.

"Excuse me!" Abby said again, pushing past Zach, Tyler, and Bethany. She wanted to hear the rest of the conversation, but she wanted to see Ms. Bunder even more.

"I'll be right back," she told Ms. Kantor, who was standing in the hallway, talking to a parent.

Yesterday Ms. Bunder had taught creative writing

class. Their assignment for the week was to take something ordinary like a lemon or a pen or a paper bag and to write about it in as many different ways as possible. Abby hadn't started yet. It sounded like fun, though. Most of Ms. Bunder's assignments were.

She ran around the corner just as Ms. Bunder came out of the library with a stack of books in her arms.

"What are you doing here?" Abby blurted out. "Are we having another creative writing class today? I hope we are!"

"I just stopped by for some books," Ms. Bunder told her. "I have to go home and work now."

"Oh," Abby said, disappointed.

"I'll tell you a secret, Abby," she said. "I'm writing a book!"

"A book!" Abby repeated. Ms. Bunder had told the class that she had published poems, a few short stories, and some articles in magazines. But a book was something else! She stared at her teacher in awe.

"It's for fifth-graders," her teacher confided. "Maybe I'll read it to the class when I'm finished."

"Yes!" Abby cried. She wondered if the book was funny or serious and whether any of the characters were based on Ms. Kantor's fifth-grade class.

"That's what I'm doing this weekend," Ms. Bunder concluded. "Working on my book. What about you?"

"Having a garage sale," Abby said.

"Wonderful!" Ms. Bunder said. "Maybe I'll stop by between chapters. I love garage sales."

"Yes!" Abby cried again. She paused. "Can I use the garage sale as the subject of my creative writing assignment?"

Ms. Bunder shifted the books in her arms. "Fifty-seven Ways to Look at a Garage Sale?" she said. "I love it!"

"Not that many!" Abby protested. "I'll never finish!"

Her teacher smiled. "Don't worry, Abby. Think of as many as you can!"

The bell rang. It was loud and final.

"We'll talk another time," Ms. Bunder said. "You'd better get back to class. See you this weekend!"

"Good-bye!" Abby wanted to talk more about the book. Would Ms. Bunder tell her about it? Sometimes writers didn't like talking about a work in progress.

Ms. Bunder waved, took a few steps, then stopped. "You'll write a book someday, too, Abby Hayes!" she called.

"Jon, Tyler, Meghan, Rachel . . ." Ms. Kantor read off the names of her class one by one. "Jessica, do you need to go to the nurse's office for your asthma medicine?"

"I already did, Ms. Kantor."

"Good," Ms. Kantor said. "Abby, Brianna, Bethany, Mason, Natalie . . ."

"Ms. Bunder's writing a book!" Abby wrote on a piece of paper and passed it to Jessica.

Jessica read the note, then wrote a few words and passed it back to Abby. She had drawn a picture of a book with legs and arms. "Maybe she'll dedicate it to us!" she had written.

"Maybe she'll base one of the characters on me or you!" Abby wrote back.

If there was a girl with curly red hair who loved to write, everyone would know who it was.

To recognize herself in a book would be amazing.

Ms. Bunder thought Abby might write a book someday, too. Was it true? Would she write her own book? Maybe Ms. Bunder would put her in a book, and she'd put Ms. Bunder in one!

Could Abby write and sell a book in a week? If so, she could skip the garage sale, the dusty attic, and sorting through piles of old clothes. She'd call Ms. Bunder and tell her the sale was off. Instead she'd become a published author on Rollerblades.

It took months or years to publish a book. By the time Abby had written and published it, Rollerblading season would be over. Should she start a book anyway? It would be good to have one ready if she ever needed it!

Chapter 13

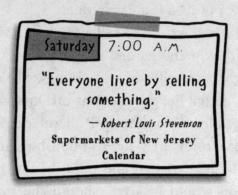

Saturday 7:00 A.M.

"Everyone lives by selling
something."
— Robert Louis Stevenson
**Supermarkets of New Jersey
Calendar**

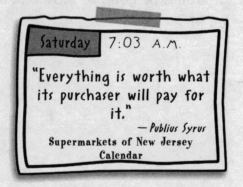

Saturday 7:03 A.M.

"Everything is worth what
its purchaser will pay for
it."
— Publius Syrus
**Supermarkets of New Jersey
Calendar**

(Two quotes for one day! Will this give
me double inspiration for my garage sale?)

What I am selling: chipped cups, plastic
dishes, stained baby blankets, worn-out

shoes, a set of plates that Mom hates, three pairs of eyeglasses, action hero under-wear, a box of comic books, dolls with weird haircuts, sweaters, old ice skates, a lamp with no shade, chewed-up baby toys, one broken lawn chair, a macramé plant holder, an old computer, a salad bowl, a 15K modem, and a jump rope. Plus a lot of other junk.

What the purchaser will pay for it: I have NO idea! (Eva is going to help me price everything.)

I went into the dark, dusty, dirty crawl space in the attic last night all by myself and brought down boxes and boxes of stuff Mom keeps forgetting to donate. Mom is grateful I am getting rid of it. She says I can keep all the money I earn, even though I didn't buy the stuff in the first place.

If I make enough money to buy Rollerblades, she promised to take me to the mall tomorrow!! HOORAY!! HOORAY!! HOORAY!!

7:15 A.M. Had fortifying breakfast of cornflakes, two jelly donuts, and pink grapefruit juice.

7:30 A.M. Set up a 50-cent table, a 75-cent table, and a $1.00 table. Bigger items (computer, dishes, ice skates) in boxes with price tags on them. Also found clothes rack to hang jackets, dresses, and shirts.

Hayes family pitched in to help. Eva priced, Dad and Isabel carried boxes, Alex posted signs in front of house. Mom arranged items on table.

8:30 A.M. Abby's Amazing Junk Jamboree Opens to the General Public!

8:32 A.M. Where is the General Public?

8:34 A.M. Forget about the General Public, where is any kind of Public?

8:36 A.M. Will start on creative writing

homework to take my mind off terrible thought: <u>What if no one comes?</u>

Five Ways to Look at a Garage Sale

1. Rugs to riches
2. A home for homeless junk
3. An untreasure island
4. A day of waiting and boredom
5. Tired, poor shoes and lamps, yearning to be free!

8:42 A.M. Customer walking up driveway!!!
8:48 A.M. First sale! Customer bought macramé plant holder for 75 cents.

8:51 A.M. No customers
8:52 A.M. ditto
8:53 A.M. ditto
8:54 A.M. ditto
8:55 A.M. Sick of writing "ditto"
9:01 A.M. Will I sit here all day?
9:02 A.M. Probably
9:06 A.M. Lots of cars parking on our

street. A neighbor's party? Hope at least one person notices garage sale.

9:07 A.M. They're all coming <u>here</u>! What do I do now? Help!!! Mommy!!!

3:13 P.M. Did entire city come to garage sale? Have been making change and saying thank you for four hours straight!

Eva helped me for an hour before lunch, then had to coach softball. I've been on my own most of the time!

Ms. Bunder came. She said she wrote two chapters of her book this morning. She was wearing jeans and a tank top and didn't look like a teacher at all.

Was embarrassed when she looked through shrunken sweaters, holey socks, and beat-up boots of Hayes family, but she bought my father's college type-writer for $5.00.

"It's practically an antique," Ms. Bunder said. She looked very pleased.

Wanted to talk more, but there

was a long line of people behind her. When I looked up again, she had gone.

Now tables almost bare. Boxes and bags gone. Money box full of coins, bills, and checks. Brain empty of thoughts, words, ideas. (It feels like lettuce in a salad spinner.)

Didn't have chance to eat lunch. Kind, thoughtful younger brother brought me peanut butter crackers and juice box a little while ago. (Will play remaining fourteen chess games owed to him. Promise!)

4:25 P.M. Tables and racks put away, trash picked up, unsold items put in bags and boxes in back of minivan.

4:33 P.M. Lunch eaten. (Almost dinnertime.)

4:48 P.M. Fed Marshmallow and changed kitty litter for second time this week.

5:05 P.M. Dad tells me I did a great job making change and helping customers.

5:06 P.M. Mom tells me I did a great job organizing and cleaning up.

5:07 P.M. Isabel says I did a great job selling her old fingernail polish.

Compliments fail to sink into brain. Too dazed and tired.

5:15 P.M. Playing chess with younger brother

5:22 P.M. Losing at chess to younger brother

5:34 P.M. Eva returns from coaching soft-ball. Asks what I got for her old Rollerblades.

I don't know what she's talking about.

"Didn't you sell the old Rollerblades?" SuperSis asks innocently.

"Sell?" I repeat. "Old Rollerblades?"

"I forgot to tell you to charge twenty dollars for them," she says.

"What???" I gasp. "I could have sold them?"

"Of course. Didn't you?"

"No!" The truth is, I never thought of it.

Eva shrugs. "I'll sell them at next year's swim team garage sale."

Could have avoided hours of hard, gruel-ing, grinding labor. Could have earned al-most all the money I needed by selling one

item only. Could have canceled garage sale
and spent day at park instead.

   5:46 P.M. Am contemplating the cruel
tragedy of life.
   "How much did you make?" Eva asks.
"If you're short a few dollars, I'll loan
them to you."
   5:47 P.M. How much money <u>did</u> I make?
Realize I put money on bed and forgot to
count it!!!

   5:56 P.M. Abby's Amazing Junk Jamboree
made $162.75!!!!!
   Is this for real?

   6:02 P.M. <u>It is</u>!!!!!
   6:03 P.M. Abby Hayes, age 10, falls
in a dead faint on the floor.
   6:04 P.M. Abby revives and dances
a jig around her bedroom.

   Don't need to borrow money from
Eva or look for more work. Can buy
new Rollerblades AND new pads!!

Chapter 14

Sunday

"Live for today."

Special Moments Calendar

Today is what I have been living for!
For the past few weeks, I have been thinking of nothing but today!

Shall I live for tomorrow, too?
Yes, because tomorrow I go to school on
new Rollerblades with purple wheels!!!

"When are we going to the mall?" Abby asked her
mother for the thirtieth time in as many minutes.

Olivia Hayes, down on her hands and knees in the
garden pulling out weeds, didn't even glance at her
watch to answer. "You know the answer to that,

Abby. The mall doesn't open until noon today. There's still at least another hour to go."

She rubbed a muddy hand across her forehead. "Why don't you help me with the yard work? Get the rake and clear off the dead leaves from the flower beds."

Abby sighed impatiently. A few days ago, she would have seen this as an opportunity to make money. Now she was rich. She didn't want to rake; she wanted to Rollerblade. *Why* did she have to wait?

"Or you can pull out dandelions," her mother suggested. "Or pick up fallen branches from the lawn. The more I get done here, the sooner we'll leave for the mall."

"Oh, all right, I guess." Anything to get to the mall quicker. At least she wouldn't have to make change. Yesterday she had made enough change to last for the rest of her life.

Abby went to find the dandelion digger. Uprooting dandelions was one of her favorite jobs. She liked digging them and trying to pull up the entire root all at once. It was more challenging than it seemed.

No matter how many dandelions she dug up each year, though, they kept coming back. Dandelions never gave up. They never seemed discouraged by the Hayes family campaign to get rid of them. Did they have inspirational calendars to give them hope? Or whole dandelion families cheering them on?

"Mom, what should I do with all my money?" Abby asked as she pushed the trowel into the earth and wiggled it around to loosen the roots of a large dandelion. "After Rollerblades, I mean."

"Put it in the bank and save it," her mother said. "That's what I would do."

"Dad told me to go on a spree."

"Your father likes to enjoy himself," Olivia Hayes said. "He'd rather throw a party or go on a trip than put money away for a rainy day."

Abby wondered why people thought money had to be put away for a rainy day. She'd rather put it away for a sunny day. That was when she wanted to swim or visit an amusement park or buy ice cream. But which of those did she *really* want to do? Could she do them all? Or would she rather get something else for her money?

Having *no* money was bad, but having money wasn't easy, either! There were too many decisions to make!

As if things weren't confusing enough, her Super-

Sibs had each given her suggestions about how to spend it.

"Isabel wants to be my investment adviser, Eva wants me to buy more tickets for her raffle, and Alex asked me to loan him money for robot parts," Abby confided in her mother.

She *had* bought an extra few raffle tickets from Eva. After all, Eva had given her two for free! But when her sister had asked her to buy even more, Abby refused.

"What do *you* want to do with it, Abby? You earned the money and should spend it the way you see fit."

Abby threw another uprooted dandelion on the brush pile. "First, buy new Rollerblades and pads. I'll have a hundred and fifteen dollars left. Then I want to . . . I want to . . . I want . . ." Her voice trailed off. "I don't know what I want! That's the problem!"

Her mother smiled. "One hundred and fifteen dollars sounds like a good problem to me. Why don't you take time to think things over? There's no rush. Don't let someone else make up your mind for you."

Her mother always gave good advice. If Abby ever needed a lawyer when she grew up, she'd hire her mother. "Okay, Mom, that's what I'll do."

She pulled out another dandelion and tossed it on the pile. It was a relief to know that she didn't have to decide what to do with her extra money right this minute. She could put it in a safe place, like a bank, or give it to one of her parents while she thought about it. Meanwhile, in an hour or two, she'd be the proud owner of new Rollerblades. Before she knew it, she'd be skating up and down the sidewalk on those shiny new purple wheels.

The dandelion pile had gotten much bigger when Abby heard footsteps coming down the walk. "Someone's here," she called to her mother.

"Oh, dear," Olivia Hayes said. "Is my face streaked with dirt?"

Abby surveyed her mother. "Not too bad, Mom. It's mostly on your hands and jeans."

As her mother brushed off the worst of the dirt, Heather came up to the fence. "Hello, hello!" she called. "Can I come in?"

As usual, she wore a handknit sweater and jeans, and in addition carried a straw basket filled with parcels. There were silver barrettes in her wild and curly hair.

They looked good. Maybe Abby could buy some

silver barrettes for *her* wild and curly hair, too.

"Of course! Come in!" Abby's mother answered. "Welcome back, Heather. How was your trip?"

"It rained the entire week," Heather said. "I had a good time, anyway."

She dug in her jeans pocket and pulled out a five-dollar bill. "I came to give Abby the rest of her money."

"Abby's been working hard lately," her mother commented.

"She took great care of Marshmallow," Heather said. "She was well fed, clean, and contented when I got back this morning."

Abby's face went red. It probably matched the color of her hair. She knew what kind of "great" care she had given Marshmallow.

Swallowing hard, she said, "I can't take the money."

"Don't be silly," Heather said. "Of course you can."

"Marshmallow escaped on Monday. I had to go to school before I found her. She stayed out all day." Abby took a deep breath. "I didn't follow your instructions. I didn't keep Marshmallow inside."

Abby didn't care if Heather didn't pay her. She just

hoped that Heather wouldn't be sorry that she had hired Abby to take care of her cat.

"Marshmallow is safe and sound," Heather said slowly. "That's what's important. I'm glad you found her, Abby, and that she was fine."

Abby took another breath. Was it true? Was it really okay she had let Marshmallow escape, as long as she had found her?

"How did you keep her inside the rest of the week?" Heather asked Abby. "I bet it wasn't easy."

"I gave her extra food and then raced to the door," Abby told her. "A couple of times she almost beat me. She streaked past me like a jet plane. Marshmallow could win races!"

"Maybe to the food bowl!" Heather laughed and held out the five-dollar bill again. "Please, Abby. You've earned it. It wasn't your fault that Marshmallow escaped. You had to bring her back, too."

"My friends came over to help me," Abby said. She took the money and put it in her pocket. "I couldn't have done it without them."

"Next time they're in the neighborhood, I'll invite them up for tea and scones," Heather said. "That's what I had in London every afternoon."

"They'll like that," Abby said. At least the girls

would. She wasn't sure about Zach, Tyler, or Mason having tea and scones. If they did, it would be one for the *Hayes Book of World Records*: Most Shocking Snacking by Fifth-Grade Boys.

Heather opened her straw bag and handed Abby's mother a package. "I brought your family tea and marmalade from England."

"What a treat!" Olivia Hayes said. "We'll enjoy this! What else did you get when you were there? Something for yourself, I hope."

"Two pounds of genuine Shetland yarn," Heather admitted. "The most beautiful shades of red. I couldn't help myself."

Abby craned her neck to read the time on her mother's watch. "It's five minutes until noon!" she announced.

"Okay, okay," her mother said. "I just have to clean myself up before we leave." She smiled at Heather. "Abby's buying new Rollerblades with the money she's earned. She wants to be at the store the minute it opens!"

"Let me guess," Heather said. "Purple?"

"Black," Abby said. "With purple wheels!"

Chapter 15

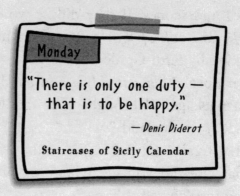

Monday

"There is only one duty —
that is to be happy."

— Denis Diderot

Staircases of Sicily Calendar

I <u>am</u> happy. Does that mean I have done my duty? <u>All</u> of it?

Do I still have to make my bed? Clear dirty dishes from the table tonight? Wipe out the bathroom sink?

I have new Rollerblades with purple wheels! I have new Rollerblades with purple wheels! I have new Rollerblades with purple wheels! I have new Rollerblades with purple wheels! I have new Rollerblades with purple wheels! I have new Rollerblades with purple wheels! (Repeat until family goes crazy.)

And a new set of pads, too.

Monday Morning Family Footwear Report
Eva Hayes: Velcro sneakers that she can fasten with her left hand only
Isabel Hayes: Platform wedge sandals
Alex Hayes: Untied sneakers with broken laces
Paul Hayes: Bedroom slippers worn with jeans and T-shirt
Olivia Hayes: Comfortable beige leather pumps with low heels
Abby Hayes: Rollerblades! Duh!!!!!!

News flash!
Abby Hayes, the wealthiest member of Ms. Kantor's fifth-grade class, showed off her new Rollerblades with purple wheels this morning on her way to school. Her classmates made many admiring comments.

Jessica said that Abby's Rollerblading skills had improved a thousand percent since she got new Rollerblades.

Natalie said the color of the wheels reminded her of an amethyst geode her brother gave her for her birthday.

Brianna said they were nice, but hers, of course, were the best that money could buy.

Bethany said, "Yay, Brianna!" But when Brianna wasn't listening, she whispered, "I think they're awesome."

Zach and Tyler asked if the brakes had "stop on a dime" technology.

Mason did not make his usual crowbar and saw remarks.

Abby Hayes skated skillfully and smoothly all the way to Lancaster Elementary. She attempted a twirl or two and did not fall down.

When she got to school, she removed her Rollerblades easily and without embarrassment. The buckles did not stick or jam. She did not have to call on her friends for help.

When she showed them to her teacher,

Ms. Kantor, she said the Rollerblades were "very impressive."

"I earned the money myself," Abby said proudly. She told Ms. Kantor about the garage sale.

"I bet you improved your math skills by making change all day," her teacher commented.

Abby Hayes amazed. Rollerblades, pads, AND better math skills? (She needs them.)

She went to her desk and took out her creative writing homework. She crossed out the title and rewrote it: "Six Ways to Look at a Garage Sale." Then she added another entry to the list: "6. Nonstop math tutorial."

Will Ms. Bunder understand? Abby Hayes will explain in complete detail if she doesn't! (Will Abby give her an idea for fifth-grade book?)

And thanks, Ms. Kantor, for helping with creative writing homework!

Abby Rollerbladed home from school with Jessica. At the corner, she waved good-bye to her best friend and flew down the street toward her house. Could life get any better?

She sat on the porch steps to take off the Rollerblades. For a moment, she admired their gleam in the sunshine. Then she flicked a speck of dust from one of the boots and gave the wheels a quick polish.

Carefully she placed them in the closet until she was ready to put them on again.

"*Very* soon," Abby promised herself. Maybe as soon as she had a snack and said hello to her father and anyone else who was around.

"I'm home!" she yelled. "Hooray! It's a great day!"

She ran into the kitchen and skidded to a halt.

Her older sister Eva was sitting alone at the kitchen table and crying.

"What's the matter?" Abby whispered. "Eva? Are you hurt?"

Slow tears dripped down Eva's face. She stared straight ahead.

"Shall I call the doctor? Or Mom? Where's Dad?" Abby asked.

"No," Eva said in a low hoarse voice. "Don't call anyone. Go away."

Abby stood in the middle of the kitchen. Now

what was she supposed to do? She couldn't just leave her sister alone, could she? Eva almost never cried. Something had to be very wrong.

"Is it your arm?"

When she didn't answer, Abby went over to the stove and found the teakettle. She filled it with water and put it on the stove. Then she pulled out the tin of tea that Heather had brought from London and took a mug decorated with bright daisies from the cupboard.

Her Grandma Emma always said a cup of tea made things better, although both her parents said they preferred coffee.

The water boiled.

"Um, can you help me pour this, Eva?" Abby said. "Otherwise I might spill it."

"My right arm is broken!" Eva cried. "I can't pour with my left. Have you forgotten?" She began to sob.

The cup of tea had made things worse, and Abby hadn't even poured it yet!

"I'm sorry, Eva. I'll pour it." She turned off the stove and picked up a pot holder. The handle was probably hot. Wasn't this how her mother did it?

With both hands, Abby picked up the kettle and poured the boiling water over a teabag in the mug.

Water splashed on the counter, but the cup filled with dark brown liquid.

She set the cup in front of her older sister.

"It's for you," Abby said. She patted her sister on the shoulder. "I hope you feel better."

Eva blew her nose and wiped her eyes. "Thanks, Abby," she whispered. She took a sip of tea. "Why am I crying?" she suddenly said. "It's only a party!"

"You're upset about your birthday?" Abby sat down across from Eva and nibbled on a cracker.

"Not mine! Susanna's." Her lip trembled. "She's having a horseback riding party and invited only seven people. I was supposed to be one of them — until I broke my arm!"

"I hate missing parties!" Abby agreed.

Eva nodded. "Especially when a boy you like is going to be there!" She looked down at her hands.

"Oh," Abby said. "Wow. Yes."

Eva had never confided in her about boys before. Her sister was too busy with sports, team events, and fighting with Isabel to even think about boys — wasn't she? Or was this something else her broken arm had changed?

"Do you think . . ." She was just about to ask her sister his name and whether Eva was inviting him to *her* party when Alex ran into the kitchen.

"Abby! There's a bunch of kids on Rollerblades outside the house! They're looking for you!"

Abby turned to her older sister.

"Go on," Eva urged. "And thanks for cheering up your SuperSib."

"You know I call you SuperSib?" Abby asked in amazement. Eva had never read her journal. Did she have X-ray vision?

"Sure." Eva smiled faintly. "Being called a Super-Sib makes me feel like I can fly. Even with a broken arm."

Eva likes a boy!!!!! I wonder who it is? An athlete with bulging muscles and a football jersey? Someone who can carry her books up and down stairs? Or her? It's too bad she has to miss the horseback riding party. And spending the day with the boy she likes.

Will be extra nice to Eva this week. Serving tea a good start. Next time remember scones and marmalade?

Chapter 16

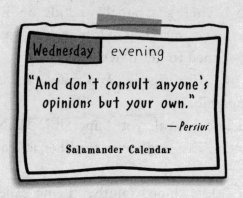

Wednesday evening

"And don't consult anyone's
opinions but your own."

— Persius

Salamander Calendar

Persius was born in A.D. 34. That's a
LONG time ago! But he gives the same advice as my mother!!!
* She always says, "Don't let someone else
make up your mind for you."

If my mother's advice is almost two
thousand years old, it must be good. It
has withstood the test of time.

What is the test of time?

Is it like a math quiz? Or a social stud-
ies test? Ms. Kantor gives us plenty of
tests! I'm glad I don't have to take the
test of time, too!!

I've decided to spend my money on my-self. And buy one small gift to cheer Eva up. She has been down in the dumps for three days.

"Down in the dumps" makes me think of rummaging in a pile of garbage, which re-minds me of the garage sale, which reminds me that Eva gave me the idea in the first place! If not for Eva, I wouldn't have all this money. So I will be _really_ nice to her. (Buy a slightly larger gift?)

But no one else! I worked at the garage sale all day. No one helped me make change or clean up the yard.

It's my money! Mine, mine, _mine_!

Dad is taking me back to mall in fifteen minutes. He says I can shop by myself as long as I check in with him every half hour.

My jeans pockets are stuffed with five- and ten-dollar bills. I will decide for my-self what I want to spend them on. New clothes? Fifteen calendars? Boxes of purple pens?

"Don't spend your money all in one place," Paul Hayes told Abby.

"Dad!" she protested. "I won't!"

"Okay, spend it in every store in the mall," he amended. "Just make sure to get the sales slips in case you change your mind later."

He gave her a quick hug. "See you in half an hour! I'll be roaming the aisles at the computer store!"

Abby waved and headed toward Edie's Earrings. Today she could buy as many earrings as she wanted. Of course, she didn't have pierced ears yet. That was a problem.

"I want to get my ears pierced," she said to the woman at the counter.

"One of your parents has to sign a consent form," the woman said, pushing a paper toward Abby. "Are they with you?"

Abby shook her head. "Maybe next time," she said. If she could convince her mother.

For now, she'd look at earrings.

There were so many earrings in the store. Silver beads, gold hoops, turquoise danglers, sparkling gemstones . . . she wanted all of them!

Would her mother change her mind if Abby showed her a drawerful of earrings?

Maybe — but probably not.

It was silly to buy earrings when she didn't have pierced ears. She already had gold hoops hidden in a box in her bureau. With one last, longing look at a pair of silver fish Abby left the store.

Next she paused in front of the clothing store where she and Jessica had encountered Brianna and Bethany. Should she buy a dress? Should she go to school dressed like Brianna and confuse the entire class?

Only if she didn't have to say "Yay, Brianna" all day long.

How much did those outfits cost, anyway? She went into the store and looked at a rack of dresses. The tags said sixty dollars, marked down from ninety dollars.

"Nope," Abby muttered. She didn't want to waste half of her hard-earned money on a dress. She didn't even like dresses.

Calendars were a sure thing. There were racks of them in the center of the mall. But which one should she buy? An Antique Candelabra calendar? Or a

Garden Decorations calendar? Or a Motor Engines calendar?

"Can I help you?" the salesperson asked, after Abby had stood in front of one rack for ten minutes.

"I can't decide," Abby said. "I like them all!"

"Get them all," the salesperson advised.

Abby shook her head. She didn't want too many at once. That was confusing! Too many calendars wouldn't make her happy; they'd give her a headache.

But which to buy? In the end, she walked away without buying a single one.

A few minutes later, she stood at a food counter and ordered a giant pretzel with chocolate sauce.

It was almost time to check back in with her father, and she'd spent a grand total of a dollar seventy-nine on a single pretzel! In a few seconds, it would be eaten. She'd have nothing to show him. Not even a gift for Eva! Some shopping spree!

At this rate, her money would rot in her pocket. She'd have to give it to her mother to put on the garden compost heap.

"Buying up the mall?" her father asked a few minutes later when she found him in the computer store. He was looking at new software programs. There was a stack of them in his shopping cart.

"No!" she cried. "I haven't bought a thing!"

Her father shook his head. "I wish I had your problems. I've already found several programs that I *have* to buy. I'm afraid I can't take my own advice," he admitted.

He patted Abby on the shoulder. "Don't worry. Even if you don't find anything today, we'll come back again."

"Sure," Abby said. "But I want to spend my money *now*."

Her father picked up another software package. "There's plenty of time. I'm not ready to leave yet. Go out and look some more."

"If nothing else, I *must* buy a gift for Eva," she told herself firmly.

In the past, she had bought her sister gifts with a sports theme. But now that she knew Eva was in love — well, she *liked* a boy — should she get her stationary with pink hearts or barrettes that said Love 4 Ever?

"Forget it!" Abby said out loud. Her sister wouldn't change *that* much.

Her eye fell on a small blue box with a picture of a space alien on its lid. It was perfect for Jessica.

"Oh, why not?" she grumbled. She didn't want to leave the mall without buying *anything*.

She paid for the gift and left the store. If she bought Jessica a gift, she might as well get one for Natalie, too. They were both her good friends. They had both helped her find Marshmallow.

She stopped in front of a stationery store. In the window, a notepad with a yellow lightbulb caught her eye.

She stared at it for a moment, then pulled her purple notebook from her backpack. In the middle of the mall, she began to write.

Ms. Bunder always says that inspiration happens unexpectedly.

She's <u>right</u>!

It happened to me just now. As I stared at the notepad, I was hit by a bolt of lightning, an idea from out of the blue.

(Question: Why are ideas compared to lightning? Why not to thunder, like rumbles in the mind?

Why do ideas come from out of

the blue? Why not from out of the <u>purple</u>?)

Back to my inspiration. Did a lightbulb turn on in my brain?

<u>Abby's Train of Thought</u> (or maybe Plane of Thought!)

1. Friends and teachers helped me find Marshmallow.

2. If cat hadn't come home, I couldn't have thrown garage sale. (Would have been too busy looking for lost pet.)

3. Without garage sale, no money.

4. Without money, no Rollerblades or pads.

5. Without friends and teachers, nothing. No cat, no blades, no money, no happiness.

Therefore (great thinkers say "therefore" at conclusion of great thoughts), <u>I should spend my extra money on thank-you gifts for the friends who helped out when I was in trouble!</u>

I'm already doing that! Maybe I was inspired and didn't even know it. Now I do!

Must continue buying presents. More, more, more! Mustn't forget my family, either. They helped with the lemonade stand and the garage sale (even if I did most of the work). They deserve presents, too!

Abby went into the store and picked up the yellow notepad with the picture of a lightbulb. Now that it had inspired her, she had to buy it. It would be the perfect gift for Ms. Bunder. She could use it to jot down book ideas!

She found a rainbow notepad for Ms. Kantor, and a pen with a thick rubber grip for Eva. It would help her with her left-handed writing. Abby wondered if Eva was planning to write love notes. Just in case, she found a stationery set decorated with lacrosse sticks and baseball stickers to seal the envelopes. Mix-and-match sports — she thought Eva would understand.

Abby paid for Eva's and her teachers' presents and loaded the bags into her backpack. She bought glittery gold nail polish for Isabel, a robot magazine for Alex, a dandelion scarf for her mother, and a Daily Bad Joke calendar for her father. She found a toy for Bethany's hamster and bought cat-shaped erasers for

Meghan, Zach, Tyler, and Mason. Last of all, she bought a magnifying glass for Natalie.

How many packages did she have now? Eight? Nine? Ten? They spilled out of her backpack and arms. She wished she had brought a suitcase!

"Looks like you had your shopping spree, after all," her father said with a smile, when she rejoined him at the computer store. "Are they all for you?"

"For my friends — " Abby stopped. She had spent all her money on friends, family, and teachers, and nothing on herself!

What had come over her? What was she thinking?

"You bought presents for your friends?" her father said. "That's very generous, Abby."

"I didn't mean to be generous," she said slowly. "It just happened."

First the space alien box and then the lightbulb notepad! They had somehow plunged her into a fever of gift-buying.

Was that how inspiration worked? Did it take you over so you forgot your normal, everyday self? Abby had been swept away on a wave of spending. At last she had reached shore again — but did she have *anything* left over for herself? She hoped so!

She patted her jeans pockets. There were still some crumpled bills there — a few dollars left for herself. That was comforting.

To tell the truth, she felt pretty good, even if she didn't have much money left. It didn't matter. Eva and Isabel's birthday was coming up soon. Abby would earn twelve dollars for baby-sitting Alex. Besides, she had new Rollerblades and pads! Beautiful, shiny Rollerblades with purple wheels and an advanced brake system. And a wheelbarrow load of presents! She couldn't wait to see the faces of her friends and family when she gave them their gifts.

Didn't say a word to Dad on way home. (Ha-ha.) He was totally surprised by his present. So was everyone in my family!

- Mother will wear scarf in court tomorrow.
- Alex disappeared to read robot magazine.
- Isabel began stripping off old nail polish to make way for new.
- Eva wrote "Thank you, Abby!" with her new pen.

— Father has vowed to tell a bad joke
every night at dinner table for next month.

News flash!
Abby Hayes has inspired her older sister,
Eva, who now plans to buy gifts for all
the basketball friends who have helped her
in school since she broke her arm.
Maybe Eva will inspire one of _her_ friends
to do the same! She will give gifts to a
group of people who have helped her. Then
one of them will be inspired and buy gifts
for another group of friends, and then one
of them will . . .
Stop, stop, stop!
End of news flash! The Roving Reporter
is dizzy from imagining entire world in
frenzy of gift-giving!

I passed my inspiration to Eva. She will
pass it to someone else.
Is inspiration a game of Telephone? Or is
it a bouncing ball that keeps going from person to person?

Must ask Ms. Bunder tomorrow in creative writing class.

Can't wait to go to school! Will give Jessica and Natalie their presents before school. Will give everyone else presents at recess, except teachers. What will they say? I bet they'll be surprised, just like my family!

Brianna will be sorry she missed Marshmallow search party. Will she want hamster ball like Bethany's? Maybe I will find brag ball for her instead.

Money spent: $62.57 in one half hour!

Records broken: <u>Hayes Book of World Records,</u> Speediest Shopping Spree by Fifth-Grader.

Goals achieved: Rollerblades with purple wheels. Hooray! Hooray! <u>Hooray!</u>

I still have more than $50.00 to spend on myself!!!

Will put leftover money in bank for a sunny day.